The Magnolia That Bloomed Unseen

The Magnolia That Bloomed Unseen

Ray Smith

UPON THE SEA BOOKS

For more information, please visit:
www.themagnoliathatbloomedunseen.com

Book design by Jason Anscomb

This paperback edition first published in 2019
www.upontheseabooks.com
Upon the Sea Books graphics designed by Freepik.com

To Mom
Of course

The
Magnolia
That
Bloomed
Unseen

PROLOGUE

RC

You've seen the woman in the photo. The woman screaming.

She is kneeling off the side of a rural road and staring directly at the camera, though this position is by accident and not by design. Even in her nondescript flannel shirt and blue jeans, she is beautiful or, at least, would be considered beautiful if society, in its infinite unwisdom, didn't deem her too old to be. Those middle-aged lines and creases, exacerbated by her distress—wide eyes, open mouth, wild hair plastered to a sweat-damp forehead—nonetheless belong to a face whose primary characteristics are beauty and courage. You can tell this is a singularly brave woman. But there are limits to the courage of even the bravest souls, and you sense that, at this moment, her courage is crushed along with everything else that she holds dear in life.

Whether the photo contains *that* everything, though, you don't know. You can't dwell on that question for you're too distracted by the rest of the photo. The other elements are too discordant, too illogical, too ugly.

The Greyhound bus behind her on the road, its shattered windows coughing out black smoke and yellow and red flames—the horrid colors of your imagination since the photo is in black and white. The dozen or so terrified blurs fleeing from the bus. The unconscious man lying on his stomach beside the woman. The circa 1960s police cruiser parked in the distance, two cops leaning complacently against it, neither helping the fire-bombed passengers but instead crossing their arms in an infuriating, what-can-we-do manner.

Ring any bells? No?

Trust me, you must've seen this photo before, maybe while flipping through the last quarter of an American history textbook. Flip fifty pages to the left and you'll see a picture of a grinning president holding up a newspaper with the wrong headline. Flip fifty pages to the right and you'll find another president, also grinning, but this grin is forced and pained, making an overhead V with his arms before he boards the presidential helicopter for the last time.

Still fuzzy? Maybe thinking I'm making this up? That's understandable. You've forgotten, that's all. And I would've too except for one little thing.

You see, I've met the woman in the photo.

Twice in my life, and each time she told me a story. The first was how she helped change the world for the better, though, in her modesty, she would never think this. And the second story saved my life. But we're getting ahead of ourselves.

Picture me now. Not as I am—a man nearing his forty-fifth birthday, with a receding hairline and a spare tire that has turned from an occasional unwelcome guest to a permanent resident around his middle. No, picture me as I was, nearly three decades ago, when a former B-movie actor was president … when I was fifteen.

Swoop down like a sparrow and see me pedaling my BMX bike from school under the great blue dome of southern California sky. I was five-six and 120 soaking-wet pounds, a nerd's nerd except I wore no glasses or braces. I was burdened by an overlarge backpack, a paralyzing shyness, and a fast-approaching deadline to an assignment.

I reached what I thought was the apartment complex, though it was hard to tell since all Laguna Hills developments looked and sounded alike: pretentious "Mediterranean" names—Venetian Villa, Tuscan Arbor, whatever—and the dull stucco walls. Still, I parked my bike outside Apartment 12D and rang the doorbell, my heart thumping in my chest. Like I've said, I was shy then—still am, really—and I was meeting my first famous person.

The woman in the photo opened the door—except she wasn't. No longer anyway. Gone was the denim-clad, middle-aged lady with the rich, dark hair. Instead, in front of me was an old woman with silver-streaked hair, and she was wearing a kitchen apron. Most different of all, she was smiling at me, an expression far removed from the horror of the picture.

My eyes processed this apparition, but my nose detected something else, emanating from the apartment. A smell like bread left in the toaster too long.

"Hi, are you, uh, Molly Valle?" I asked.

"Sure. You're Susan's student, right?"

It took me a moment to wonder who Susan was, then I guessed it must've been the first name of Ms. Jankowski, my history teacher. The one who'd told me about an old teaching colleague, a civil rights hero who would gladly talk about her experiences for my final history assignment, a biographical sketch of a real-life hero.

"Yes, Ms. Jankowski told me I could, uh, interview you and—"

"Sure, come on in. Make yourself at home. I'll be right back."

With that, she spun on her heels and disappeared into the apartment with a speed surprising in such an old body. But, then again, to a teenager, anyone over forty seemed capable of reading hieroglyphics. I stepped inside.

The apartment was small and cluttered, but it also had a comfortable, lived-in feel to it. Hanging from the walls was artwork and even my fifteen-year-old eyes could tell she hadn't picked up the pieces from the local swap meet.

There were African masks, European oils, Asian watercolors, and various figurines whose origins I could no more work out than how to win over the cute cheerleader in Geometry 1B. Then there were the books. They weren't so much stacked on the mismatched bookshelves as overrunning them like Mongols over enemy fortifications, with more than a few lying on the carpet like poleaxed soldiers. And incongruously, on one bookshelf amidst the chaos, was a wood-framed picture of a smiling, large-featured man who resembled an actor in those French movies my mom was always watching. Her son?

"So, what's your name again?" Ms. Valle called from the kitchen, of which I could only glimpse a section from where I stood in the living room. She appeared like a frantic shadow moving here and there, backlit by an orange glow. Flames?

"RC, ma'am," I called out as I sat down on a couch. "Like the cola."

"RC? That's certainly unique. Why are you called that?"

"Those are the initials of my first and middle names."

"Makes a lot of sense to me. Would you like something to drink? I'm almost done here."

"No thanks, ma'am," I said, though I doubted she was almost done. And I was right. It would be five more minutes before she left the kitchen, her apron smeared and her hair spiked up, looking like a Warner Bros cartoon villain after the ACME bomb had blown up in her face. She set a tray of cookies and a glass of milk in front of me then collapsed in her own seat.

After I'd thanked her, she smiled and said, "You know, when I retired from teaching, I thought my stress levels would go down. But next to cooking, I'd take a classroom of freshmen any day of the week."

I nodded like I knew what she was talking about. "What were you making?"

"Something French. I don't want to butcher the name any more than I did the recipe."

It *was* Molly Valle sitting across from me. This I could see now. On closer inspection, there was enough resemblance—the high cheekbones, the shape of her eyes—to convince me that this old lady and the middle-aged woman in the photo were the same person.

The expression "don't judge a book by its cover" was apt, but the distance between the civil rights hero and this woman defeated by a cooking recipe was far too wide. Later, much later, I would learn Molly's philosophy of finding the extraordinary behind the everyday, which was itself, on the surface, a hoary cliché. But it was also a truth I never fully grasped, especially not as a foolishly gaping fifteen-year-old.

"So, RC," Ms. Valle said, "what do you want to know?"

"Everything, I guess."

"Everything's a tall order, kiddo."

"Then maybe enough for me to get an A in Ms. Jankowski's history class."

The old lady smiled. "Now, you're talking."

And she did tell her story, the CliffsNotes version anyway. Being born in Mississippi in 1912 and growing up there. Being an English teacher during the early 1960s when the civil rights workers arrived in her small town. Being fired from her job due to her involvement with the so-called outside agitators. Her involvement with the Freedom Riders and being on the bus that was firebombed in Alabama in 1961, which resulted in the famous photo. Her sense of triumph after civil rights were finally given to African Americans in the South, and her subsequent move to southern California to start a new life and a new teaching job, which she kept until her retirement five years earlier at the age of sixty-eight.

"I figured I'd given enough of my life to education," Ms. Valle said, "so I've been tooling around the world these last couple of years." Her eyes swept across the apartment filled with curios. "Would that be enough for your paper?"

"More than enough," I said and looked up from my scribbling. "Thank you."

"Well, then, I'm glad to have helped," she said and stood up. "I guess you can find the rest at the library, but if you need any more help, just give me a ring. Okay, RC?"

I nodded, but I didn't need to call her back. Even before the age of the internet, it was a cakewalk finding information on the civil rights era from microfiche. I wrote my paper, titled, during a burst of unimaginable creativity, "Molly Valle: Civil Rights Hero," and received an A. Ms. Jankowski was so pleased, she even nominated me for Student of the Month, the first and last time my slacker self ever received that honor. My parents took me on that grand tour of nerd celebration—pizza followed by miniature golf—and later, after Ms. Jankowski suggested I show Ms. Valle my paper, I returned to Apartment 12D right before summer break.

"Most excellent, RC," Ms. Valle said, taking off her reading glasses after looking over my paper. She looked less flustered today, which was probably explained by her ordering Chinese takeout instead of cooking. "So, you ever thought of writing for a future?"

I hesitated then nodded. "I thought of majoring in English then becoming a novelist."

"You definitely should, kiddo. You have talent."

I nodded, but I wasn't looking at her. For some reason, I found myself staring at the portrait of the man on the bookshelf.

"Who's that?" I blurted out.

Ms. Valle didn't seem surprised I'd asked the question. She didn't even turn around to see whom I meant.

"A very talented man I knew a long time ago," she told me. "Someone who gave me a recipe once."

"To that, uh, French dish?"

"Yes, and he made it a lot better than I could." A brief pause. "And he gave me a recipe to something else too."

"What's that?"

"Life," she said and smiled. But the smile seemed sad. "God, that came off so pretentiously, didn't it? It's true, though. But that's one story I won't be telling today."

I nodded, but I didn't know what she was talking about. And it wasn't the only strange statement she made that afternoon. As she escorted me to the door, she asked me, "Did any of your teachers tell you that your high school years will be the best of your life?"

I nodded again. In fact, three had: Mr. Spaulding, the assistant principal; Mr. Lowell, my English teacher; and Mr. Chang, my PE teacher. Many years later, I wondered why it'd only been male teachers who'd told me this.

"Don't believe them," she said, and there was an insistence in her voice. "Whatever excitement you feel right now in life, at fifteen, don't ever let it escape. Grab onto it and hold tight, even if it's bucking and biting and tearing at you to get away. Promise me that."

"I promise," I said, though I hadn't the slightest inkling what she meant. Then and later, when I no longer called her Ms. Valle but Molly, she often said things I didn't fully understand, to my detriment.

However, I did understand her parting words to me that afternoon three decades ago because they filled me with a giddy warmth:

"Keep in touch, RC. You're meant for great things."

I didn't keep in touch. I meant to, but life—school, girls then women, jobs, taxes—got in the way. And I didn't keep my promise.

I lost the "excitement" Ms. Valle had talked about, but, in my defense, her analogy wasn't exactly apt. For excitement wasn't a wild animal you held on to but a quality that languidly leaked from your life like air from a balloon. Not abruptly but gradually with each passing year as my twenties shifted to my thirties and then dissolved into my forties. By the time I was nearing forty-five, life had all the unpredictability and adventure of a microwavable TV dinner, which I actually often ate in my small apartment in Los Angeles.

My only consolation was that my friends' lives weren't any different. I looked at them—single, married, divorced, it made no difference—and I observed the same incipient gray hairs and the same long-established gray lives. Over twenty years earlier, my college roommate had boasted that he was going to rent a yacht with fifty hookers and sail the Caribbean, but now he, like so many others, was a cubicle dweller, and the extent of his dream's realization was emailing me the occasional sailing video he liked on YouTube.

What happened to us? To *all* of us?

Needless to say, I never became a writer. At least, not one of any consequence. Just a few published short stories. No published novels, no produced screenplays. I had planned to be married to a brilliant, beautiful woman by thirty-five, but I was still single and childless nearly a decade later, with an impressive number of collapsed relationships behind me. And I had become a high school English teacher just like Ms. Valle. But, unlike her, I knew it wasn't my calling and always approached summer vacations like an overboard *Titanic* passenger flailing for a lifeboat.

I was just beginning one of those blessed summers, sweating over a story on my laptop because my apartment's air-con had given up the ghost again, when my iPhone rang. I didn't recognize the number.

"Hello?"

"Hello, RC, how are you?" came the female voice, weak and raspy.

RC. I hadn't been called that since I left for college over a quarter-century ago. And for some miraculous reason, I knew who it was in an instant.

"Ms. Valle!" I said, glad to hear her—and the surprise in my own voice since my life had long been drained of surprises. "How are you?"

"I'm fine," she said, then there was a pause. "Actually, life lately hasn't exactly been a bowl of cherries."

She talked, and I listened. The fact that I was speaking to her finally hit me. I remembered her, as the saying went, like it was just yesterday, but "yesterday" was really thirty years ago. She was now 103 years old, a detail that momentarily short-circuited my synapses. When they recovered, I heard her telling me she was still living at home and, outside of traveling, was still enjoying the same hobbies she had always enjoyed.

"Like reading. I read your stories, RC. I always knew you would be a writer."

"Thank you," I said, wondering how she'd found them. My short stories had all been published in literary magazines with room-temperature circulations.

"But I wouldn't call myself a writer," I went on, "more of a wannabe writer."

"Oh, no, you're a writer. Don't doubt yourself." There was a pause. "In fact, how would you like to hear another story from me? Maybe one you might be interested in writing."

I was thrown for moment. "Sure, okay. What is it about?"

"The man in the photo."

Don't know how I remembered, but I did. The photo on the cluttered bookshelf. The guy who resembled a French actor, except I now knew the performer's name since my mom had dragged me to see *Green Card* in 1990, four years after first meeting Ms. Valle. The man in the photo looked like a middle-aged Gerard Depardieu.

Ms. Valle was speaking again: "I was being disingenuous when I said he only gave me a French recipe."

"You said he gave you a recipe to life too."

"Did I? Guess my memory's really going, huh? But I'm sure whatever mistakes I make in telling my story, you can always check up on Google later, right? The dates, at least, if nothing else."

That was the truth. Months later, after she'd told me what she could of her tale, I double-checked everything. Through Google, the library, interviews, and even trips to her hometown in Mississippi. By then, the research had become an obsession—a life-affirming and life-altering one—for I knew I had to bring the story before the world, even if that was the last thing I did with my life.

At that moment on the phone, however, these events were all ahead of me.

"Okay, I could come by to hear it," I said, thinking I'd indulge an old lady's request. She did help me get an A in history class, after all. "When are you free?"

"How about tomorrow morning?"

Which was abrupt, but I said yes anyway. That was Sunday, June 5th, 2016—two years, ten months, and seventeen days ago. The next morning, Monday, June 6th, 2016, she began telling me the second story, the one that you have in front of you now.

The story that changed my life and, if I were to wager a gentleman's bet, maybe change yours too.

Spring 2019

CHAPTER 1

1961
JOHN

"Never thought I'd get so nervous getting a cup of coffee."

"That's just the thing, now, isn't it? You shouldn't be nervous. Nobody should."

"Yeah, I guess not," William said and nodded, but to John Pressman, he didn't look convinced. John, steering, thought his young passenger looked like he was about to yank open the door and dive out of their Rambler rolling by on the highway at forty miles an hour.

William Graham—always William, never Bill or Will—was wearing his usual crisply ironed suit and gold-rimmed glasses, and appeared as he always did, like someone applying for a job straightening papers at an insurance adjuster's office. But his rigid sitting posture was *too* rigid, and even with the near-blinding sunshine spilling through the windshield, he didn't squint or hardly even blinked.

He's just a kid from Wisconsin, John thought. A kid who wanted to help change the world but whose desire had long been abstract. Now, however, with the Mississippi summer compressing their bodies inside the car and the encircling forest, sickly in its pungency, pinning and directing them to a seeming execution, the original want had been given a terrible, tangible reality. William had never known what he was getting himself into.

John felt his own fear uncoiling inside his chest. *Do* you *know what you're getting yourself into?* He wasn't sure, but he knew one thing: he'd better do something before the young man fell apart.

"Here's the thing," John found himself saying. "If you've never had coffee before, its bitterness is going to hit your tongue like battery acid the first time you try it."

William turned to him. "What are you talking about?"

"Coffee. You said getting it gives you the willies, didn't you? Well, I'm here to tell you how you can deal with it."

William said nothing in reply, but his unblinking, non-squinting eyes finally did blink and even approximated a squint under the weight of an emerging frown. The fear was still there but now had to share his face with other emotions: confusion, incredulity, even distaste.

"Get some cream, get some sugar," John told him, "and approach it like a wizard concocting a magic potion. Add nine-tenths cream and sugar and one-tenths coffee at first, and gradually increase the coffee content. Who knows? If you settle on the right combination, you might even market it and become a millionaire. Call it the Elixir of Getting Up Without Throwing Up." As an encore, John grinned as widely and stupidly as he could.

One second, two, then three. On William's countenance, fear was in the tug-a-war with confusion and distaste, but all were losing badly to disbelief, which had grown to a Charles-Atlas size and muscularity. *Good, very good.*

"John," William finally said, and he even smiled, though haltingly. "You know I wasn't talking about being afraid of the *taste* of coffee, right?"

"Of course, he knows."

John glanced into the rearview mirror and saw Bethanee Avery shaking her head at him from the backseat. She'd stayed so quiet since they'd left Jupiter Hammon College fifteen minutes earlier, he had almost forgotten she was there, which was extraordinary.

Only twenty, a year younger than even William, and slight of build, Bethanee nonetheless had a presence, whether in her unwavering brown-eyed gaze or her deep, throaty voice, which sounded more like it belonged to a cigarette-abusing crosswalk guard than to what she really was: a college sophomore studying English literature. Even her fashion sense, deliberately outdated to recapture Jazz Age pizazz, was indelible: a white and blue flapper's sailor blouse with matching cloche hat—under perfectly bobbed hair, of course.

"He just toying with you," Bethanee told William, and scooted up till her skinny forearms rested on the backrest between John and the younger man. "Getting your mind off what you about to do."

John noticed Bethanee's voice had changed again. Whenever she was alone with him, she used her usual accent, a bland Americana of indistinguishable origin. Around William and some others, however, she adopted this embellished Southern voice, though not always successfully. Contrived even.

"Yes, I understand that," William told her and gulped. "But I'm not sure if it worked."

Bethanee slapped his shoulder. "Don't you worry about a thing. Mama's here to protect you."

As if in challenge to her assertion, the forest slowly thinned and the town's outskirts came into view, its multicolored boxes—gas stations, liquor stores, diners—intruding on the previously unblemished, all-enveloping green. The traffic around them thickened too, and when John looked into the rearview mirror, he could no longer spot the Studebaker and the Ford that housed the six other volunteers. Instead, a rust-flaked Chevy pickup was tailgating them, and then a police cruiser sped by on their left, which caused even Bethanee—John saw this in the rearview—to tense for a second. He could smell the cop car's exhaust and also William's fear, like the scent of spoiled lemons.

Where are the others? John thought and began to scratch the scar on his chin, which had begun to itch, as it always did whenever he was apprehensive.

The three stayed quiet as John steered their car off the highway. The street dipped, and once they'd crested a hill, a tourist's postcard of an idyllic Mississippi town presented itself, from the lime hills that housed the magnificent antebellum mansions to the two cantilever bridges that chalk-lined across the Mississippi River in the distance. Under the limitless azure of the sky was the downtown of church spires, brownstone facades, and ironwork balconies, less a historical Southern downtown of reality but of a fantasy.

It was, John decided, the kind of breathtaking view that should've been accompanied by birdsong and the fragrance of magnolias and gardenias.

But he never placed much faith in the surface of things, for the reality of most everything went below its shell, far below. From countless experiences, he knew the most prosaic facades often hid the greatest beauty, but most people missed this fact because they never looked hard or long enough to truly *see*.

Conversely and sadly, John also knew the most beautiful vistas often hid the ugliest truth. The exquisite face that obscured the rotten soul. The opulent brownstone with the termite-gutted frame. The stunning Mississippi town built by slave labor and maintained by Jim Crow.

No, things were never what they seemed.

"Emerald of the Mississippi, my ass," Bethanee said, breaking the silence. Emerald of the Mississippi—the town's unofficial nickname, though now, John thought with a smile, with an added tagline. Yes, Bethanee glimpsed below the surface of things too, but then folks like her always did. They *had* to.

They were in the heart of downtown. Red-brick storefronts, gleaming windows, green awnings. John slowed and parked the Rambler by the curb, their destination a half-block away. Through the open windows, he heard happy, oblivious chatter and, from somewhere, the aroma of fried onions. A lot of people walking—

maybe *too* many people—and if it weren't for the gravity of what they were about to do, John would've lingered in the car just to see the pedestrians' expressions when they saw him being a veritable chauffeur to Bethanee and William.

"You scared, Bethanee?" William asked, his voice high-pitched enough to sing an aria.

"Not at all. Figure the worst thing that could happen is we wind up in the hospital with a few broken bones, but last time I checked, the human body's got over two hundred." She turned to her left. "Look at John. He ain't afraid none."

John, whose heart was thumping rather spiritedly, said nothing.

"Of course, he's got something that you and I don't got," Bethanee told William.

John saw William tense beside him.

"His lucky charm watch, I mean," Bethanee added and chuckled.

John rubbed his wristwatch, an heirloom from his father, and bit his tongue. He knew she didn't mean his watch, and he knew William knew it too. He didn't feel anger but an inexact pity for Bethanee. He wondered if her current discourtesy had anything to do with what'd happened a couple nights earlier, when she'd gone into his room in only her nightgown and he had rebuffed her. It wasn't that she wasn't desirable but rather she was far too young for him. The fact that some women did find him attractive he always considered a minor miracle since he'd never considered himself handsome.

But he pushed these ruminations away and turned to his young colleagues. "You two know the plan?"

"Where are the others?" William asked and craned his head back. "Where are they?"

John turned around too and looked back up the street. In the wavy, mid-morning heat, there was a phalanx of cars but no blue Studebaker or brown Ford. The three waited a moment. Then, rounding the corner a block away, the two cars appeared at last. The cavalry. The *unarmed* cavalry.

Still, he breathed a sigh of relief and turned back to Bethanee and William. "Okay. Come in five minutes after I do. You two got it?"

Two nods, and Bethanee put her hand on his shoulder. "Sorry for razzing you, John. Good luck, okay?"

"Sure, we'll be okay," John said, but he wasn't certain he meant it. He opened the door, hesitated a split-second, then stepped out of the car.

The Mississippi sun felt like a heat lamp held an inch from his face. He blinked, wiped his sweat-beaded forehead, and started toward his destination: a set of double glass doors set into a brick storefront under a sign proclaiming, "The Porky Pie." According to guidebooks, it was the most popular diner downtown. Nearing lunch hour, it should be packed, which was why the organization had picked it in the first place. Maximum impact. He, along with Bethanee and William and the six other volunteers, would be the first infantry storming the beachhead.

He walked casually, and nobody gave him a second glance. Nobody, that was, except two old ladies who did look at him a bit too long as he passed. He wasn't sure what they were staring at until he realized he'd forgotten to cut his hair. His hair, mostly blond but graying at the temples, was too long for a man pushing fifty-one in this town. Maybe too long for *any* age here.

He paused at the diner entrance and took one more look around. There—he spotted three men standing across the street, observing him. He didn't recognize them, but he felt no unease either. The organization had called them, even though they weren't volunteers. All three were middle-aged men, wearing dark, too-hot suits with bulges in them, and all sported the same pale faces, untouched by a full day of sunshine under the Mason-Dixon Line. One even smiled and nodded at him, as if encouraging him forward.

But John needed no prompting as he turned, opened the doors, and stepped inside the diner. Blessedly cold air sheathed his body, and his ears picked up the sizzle of meats and onions on the griddle a split-second before his nose made out their delicious smells. Nearing lunch hour, the place *was* packed, full of office workers and clerks from nearby businesses. Behind the counter, a young rumpled waitress took orders and a large teenage boy, struggling under a precipitous stack of dirty dishes, disappeared into the back room.

"Say, buddy, mind if you shut the door? You're letting the heat in," someone to his left said, and John did as instructed.

He made his way into the diner, past the jam-packed red booths to the far end of the counter, where he'd spotted an empty stool. He sat down and took the menu from its holder, feeling his heart thumping again. To lull it, he turned to the woman sitting to his left and asked, "So, what do you recommend for lunch here?"

The woman turned to him, and he observed she was someone his own age or a bit younger. Dark, wavy hair and large brown eyes behind schoolmarm glasses. A friendly, olive-complected face. Not stereotypically Southern, if there was such a thing. Greek or Spanish maybe. He wasn't sure.

What he did know was that he felt something then. Something that was shapeless and intangible, but neither quality made it—whatever it was—any less *there*. It was a shifting of his senses or maybe even of reality itself. You turned a corner and a stunning landscape presented itself, and though you yourself had not changed, everything else had for, after you'd seen this new thing, whatever this thing was, you automatically understood the mechanisms of life could not go back to where they had been before. The sight—though it could more properly be called an experience, encompassing all five senses and even ones not yet discovered—rendered everything before it monochrome and matte.

John Pressman had only felt this way twice before in his life with a woman, and this time, he felt it at fifty years, four months, and twenty-three days of age. At a greasy spoon in a small town in Mississippi in the summer of 1961.

"Try the country-fried steak," the woman said and smiled. "It's the best in three counties."

CHAPTER 2

MOLLY

An hour earlier, roughly a mile and a quarter away as the crow flew—or, more appropriately, as the mockingbird flew, for that was Mississippi's state bird—this same woman was sitting in her own kitchen. Her house was in a twenty-acre rectangle of postwar tract homes built just south of downtown, far from the Doric-columned mansions that lined the bluffs above the river but just as equally far from the shotgun shacks where the coloreds lived *far* north of the center. In her neighborhood, there were well-kept but not manicured lawns, late-model but not too-new cars, and, most importantly, mortgages that a single-income teacher could afford.

And forty-eight-year-old Molly Valle, in a patterned housedress and eyeglasses, looked very much the teacher, especially when she stabbed a pencil at the textbook on the tabletop and told the boy sitting across from her to look at the passage again.

"So who doesn't abandon Everyman in the end?" Molly asked.

"Good Deeds, right?" the boy said, though to call him a boy was to stretch the word to its breaking point. Although only sixteen, Cash Harper was a mountain of a boy, who, in his too-tight clothes, always appeared like a professional wrestler constricted inside a Boy Scout's uniform.

"That's right," Molly said. "Everyone abandons Everyman except Good Deeds."

The boy ruminated a second then said, "But wouldn't Knowledge go with Everyman too after death? I mean, we're still reading Shakespeare, aren't we? And he's been pushing up daisies for hundreds of years now."

She laughed. "You've got a good point there, but I don't think realism was on the minds of writers of sixteenth-century morality plays. This isn't *Rebel Without a Cause*."

"Got it. That wasn't too tough, Miss Vail."

Miss Vail, Molly thought. That was how people had pronounced her last name since she was a little girl. The *incorrect* pronunciation.

But she didn't bother to correct her student and instead said, "No, it wasn't. Students often make a big deal out of literature, but really, these people weren't much different from you and me, even if they wrote funny. You'll see, once we start on Transcendentalism this winter."

"Transcendent—what?"

"Transcendentalism," Molly said and stood up. She went to the counter, arranged a small plate of cookies, placed it on the tabletop, and sat down again. "Don't worry. If you need help, I'm always available for tutoring."

Cash's eyes lit up at the cookies, and he took one. "Thanks, Miss Vail. But I'm gonna have football practice once school starts. I also got that new job I was telling you about."

Molly nodded and looked at the guileless, happily chewing face of the enormous boy whom she'd known almost from birth. While his body seemed tailor-made for punishing sports, she also knew his mind was built for something else—math and science and their precise yet unbounded mysteries. He'd once expressed to Molly his wish to become an engineer but then immediately retracted it as if it were a shameful admission. In this town, any boy with Cash Hopkins's physique was never meant to be an engineer.

Her reflections were interrupted, however, by a triplet of honks from the street. "Oh, that's me," Cash said, got his backpack from the floor, and unceremoniously swept his English literature textbook and notebook inside.

Molly followed the boy out the front door. Under the late-morning sun, she felt the heat not only as a steam press on her skin but also as a cloying nothingness that pushed into her nostrils. Summer itself seemed to possess a torrid, unsated anger. She raised her hand to shield her squinting eyes and blinked once. When she blinked again, she saw a police cruiser broiling on her driveway. The driver's door opened, and Cash's identical twin stepped out.

Except this twin was three decades older. Same height and circus-strongman body, though the stomach spilled over the leather belt. Same pink, sunburned face, and when the man took off his sunglasses, same pale blue eyes. Then the illusion broke as he, displaying none of Cash's gentleness, slammed the car door and took off his hat, revealing a scalp completely denuded of the straw-colored hair on the boy's head.

"Morning, Molly," Hollis Harper said. "This is what I've been reduced to—driving my boy around like some colored help. You know, Cash, back in the day, we had these contraptions with wheels on them that we called bikes."

"Thanks, Daddy," the boy said, opened a rear car door, and threw his things in.

"Thanks nothing. Boy, if you was half as good in English as you are in biology"—Hollis stretched out the word into five, distasteful syllables: *bi-o-ah-lo-gee*—"you wouldn't always be bothering Miss Molly none."

"He's okay," Molly said and winked at Cash. "He's finally got a handle on *Everyman*."

Hollis smiled an uncertain smile then yawned. Molly decided he'd long forgotten the morality play they used to study together in 11th-grade English. She guessed that he could be excused since that was over three decades ago.

"Hotter than a goat's butt in a pepper patch," Hollis mumbled and mopped his forehead. When he wiped his wet hand onto his shirt, the action added another sweat patch to a dozen already visible. He looked less a chief of police than an over-the-hill army recruiter in blue camouflage.

"You look tired, Hollis," Molly said.

"I am that. Spent half of last night at a town hall calming folks down. Whole town's got ants in their pants about those outside agitators everyone keeps reading about in the papers. I told everyone they ain't come yet, but rest assured, the police department's gonna be in fighting trim if they do." Hollis let out another yawn. "Never seen you in none of those meetings, Molly."

The "outside agitators" had indeed been all over the papers, and though she wasn't sure how she felt about them, she never understood any of the visceral fulminations of her neighbors and friends.

So she found the lie easy. "I've been busy. Planning lessons and such. A teacher's life." To buttress her point, she glanced over and smiled at Cash. The boy, standing patiently by the cruiser's passenger door, had become a silent spectator to the adults' conversation.

"Planning lessons? Didn't the school year just end?" Hollis chuckled. "On second thought, that sounds about right. I always pegged you as the studious one in high school."

"That's me in a nutshell," Molly said but thought, *No, Hollis, that's not how you saw me in high school.*

She remembered him, from junior high onwards, sneaking peeks at her legs whenever they sat near each other. And the stammering, glance-averted way he'd speak to her whenever they passed each other in their high school hallways. Most of all, she recalled the devastating collapse of his features when he had finally summoned the courage to ask her out and discovered she was already dating Adrian McCluey, the tuba player in Instruments 10B.

But that was geological periods ago, when she was a slender girl with the rich black hair that Pocahontas would've envied and the sun-browned legs that fit her Sears Roebuck shorts just right. A million years, twenty-odd fewer pounds, dozens of fewer wrinkles, and a few stray gray hairs ago.

No, Hollis, Molly thought, *you're not the only one who's aged. You're just lucky enough to have the power of reincarnation in your son.* And in those thirty years that separated Hollis's and Cash's physical transformations, Molly found that she too—and she'd imagine, plenty of women her age—had developed a magical ability, albeit an unwelcome one: the power of invisibility.

"Well, I guess that's that. Take care, Molly." Hollis put his hat back on. "Say goodbye to Miss Molly, Cash."

"Goodbye, Miss Vail." Cash opened the passenger door. "Thanks for all your help. If it gets too hot here, you can always visit me at work. Old Man Stoddard just got some air-conditioning installed."

"Fancy that," Molly said, taken aback. Old Man Stoddard was the ancient, parsimonious fixture who owned The Porky Pie diner, where Cash had his new busboy/dishwasher job.

Hollis chuckled. "Yeah, I was surprised too. Old Man Stoddard always did squeeze a nickel till the buffalo crapped, excuse my French."

The town's chief of police was still chuckling as he, with his lookalike son sitting beside him, reversed his cruiser out of Molly's driveway, and then, with a wave of his hand, drove off into the heat-rippling distance.

What now? Molly thought as she went back inside and collapsed onto her living room sofa. Even indoors, it was still crushingly hot, and despite its small size, barely a thousand square feet, the house felt empty, like an abandoned Mojave Desert shack she'd seen in a *Life* magazine article. Her home even *sounded* empty, as if the outside world's cheerful sounds didn't want their cheerfulness diminished by the barrenness within her walls.

During the school year, she often worked late in her classroom and attended functions so she never had time to dwell on how lonely she'd become. She was too blessedly tired. Still, when summer began, she wondered why she hadn't already gone to the pet store to get a dog or a cat or even a turtle. Of course, she had never felt more alone than when she was married, a good decade earlier. This current loneliness, however … well, it couldn't be lifelong, could it? But with each new year alone, the answer seemed an ever colder, more certain yes.

Thankfully, her empty stomach prevented her from dwelling on these thoughts further, and it was too hot to cook. What was Truman's favorite saying? *If you can't stand the heat, get out of the kitchen.* Remembering what Cash had said, Molly decided to not only get out of the kitchen but out of her house altogether. After a cold bath, a dab of makeup, and a change of clothes—a pastel blue dress with a full skirt to contain her increasingly rebellious butt—she was out the door and in her seven-year-old Plymouth heading downtown.

Fifteen minutes later, she had parked and was stepping inside The Porky Pie, the cold air causing her to feel like an Eskimo returning to the North Pole from a Central American rainforest. Not that— Molly smiled at her own image—she'd been to either location.

The place was packed as usual, and she relished its familiar aromas as she made her way to the end of the counter, which held the only free seats. Around half of the diners she passed she recognized to some extent—when you were a teacher in a small town, you got to know folks—and she smiled and nodded to them. They returned in kind. All except for a loud group of young men whose faces Molly vaguely remembered from an appalling 9th-grade class a dozen years ago. And three middle-aged men who sat together in a booth, their too-dark, heavy suits showcasing their out-of-town status.

Traveling salesmen? she wondered.

As she sat down at the counter, she spotted Cash coming out from the swinging doors that led to the kitchen. He was wearing a too-small white uniform with a too-small white apron. On him, the getup looked like a straitjacket whose sleeves had been cut off.

"Hi, Miss Vail!" he called out upon seeing her.

Molly smiled. "Guess I made it, after all."

"You like the cold, don't you?" Cash picked up an impressively tall stack of dirty dishes. "Talk later!" he said as he hurried back into the kitchen.

Molly said hello to the waitress—Peggy Ellis or Ferris, 11th-grade American Lit, six or seven years ago—ordered a vanilla Coke, and studied the menu. She became aware of a man sitting down on the empty stool next to her and had just about decided on the patty melt, diet be damned, when she heard him ask, "So, what do you recommend for lunch here?"

When she turned to the man, she observed he wasn't anyone she'd seen before, and she'd bet he wasn't local either. Nor was he one of the dark-attired traveling salesmen. No, he was casually dressed in a striped polo shirt and tan pants, and his blond, partly graying hair was too long for his age—late forties, early fifties? He looked a bit like an aging beatnik, and other than an inch-long slice of a scar on his chin, his face was unremarkable.

Except it wasn't. For as Molly looked at him, she felt an immediate … she didn't know what. Despite her love of the language arts, she also possessed an analytic mind, and that mind straightaway tried to seek out the *why*. And it couldn't unearth the reason apart from his smile. Or, rather, *how* he smiled at her—warm and full-armed, like the embrace from a long-absent friend, without the slightest trace of fakeness or concealed motive.

His was the most open face she'd ever seen in her life.

Concomitant with these sensations, all delivered within a split second, was a thought, seemingly originating not in her mind but from the center of her torso and radiating out to the ends of each nerve, inexplicable in its suddenness and surety. A thought that children and very young people might have, but never middle-aged adults, especially one with a divorce behind her and the conviction that she already knew the world and what it was able to offer.

But there it was, undeniably, the thought: *I'm on a great adventure.*

"Try the country-fried steak," she said in response to his question. "It's the best in three counties."

It was 12:34 p.m. and forty-three seconds on a summer afternoon in 1961, in a busy diner in small-town Mississippi. Floyd Patterson was the heavyweight champion of the world. Bobby Lewis's "Tossin' and Turnin'" ruled the charts. The young Irish-American president was safe and sound in the White House. And for Molly Valle, forty-eight-year-old schoolteacher, life had just changed forever.

One second later, at precisely 12:34 p.m. and forty-four seconds, her town also changed forever.

Because a young man, neatly dressed in a pressed suit and wearing gold-rimmed glasses, walked inside The Porky Pie, his skin glistening with nervous sweat. As he stumble-walked deeper into the diner, a twenty-foot bubble of silence encircled him. Then he sat down on the empty stool to the blond man's right and even smiled at him. But it was the smile of a man ascending the steps to the guillotine.

Molly, whose heart seemed to have stopped, guessed that was the appropriate reaction.

The young man was a Negro, after all.

CHAPTER 3

MOLLY

"I would like a cup of coffee," Molly heard the young man ask Peggy the waitress. His words were hesitant and stumbling, and his hand shook as he picked up the menu.

A cup of coffee. A perfectly reasonable request from someone sitting at the counter of a diner. The most natural request in the world but so, so wrong coming from *this* man.

It was so wrong that Molly, still staring at him, hadn't noticed she was sliding off her stool. She caught herself as she stumbled off—she would forever be ashamed of this movement—and as she stood unsteadily, a young black woman took her seat. This girl was dressed so oddly, in what looked like flapper clothes—blue cloche hat with matching blue sailor blouse—Molly blinked to make sure she was real. She was, and so were the young black man and the middle-aged blond guy. All three just sat nonchalantly next to each other.

As if nothing groundbreaking was happening at all, Molly marveled. But, of course, something was. Everything was.

She felt the unreality of the situation then. Hollis Harper's warnings and the newspaper stories about the "outside agitators" had come to life, and she felt transported into the world of newsprint. Gone were the greasy smells from the griddle and the happy banter of the diner. Her taste buds and skin likewise seemed to register no sensation. Of her senses, only sight remained, and that was solely focused on the lunch counter as more regulars, like sailors bailing from a sinking ship, eased themselves off their stools, only to be immediately replaced by more young strangers. Most of these were black, but there were a few whites as well, and each reached for the menu and asked Peggy the waitress for a cup of coffee.

Molly heard movement behind her, and when she turned her head, she saw just about everyone in the diner had been shocked still. All except those three dark-suited strangers who, as if by an unspoken signal, removed cameras from beneath their coats, and Molly thought, *Of course.* Of course, of course, of course.

They weren't traveling businessmen but reporters, maybe even among those who'd taken the photos that graced her local paper. Photos of other cities, true—Greensboro, Nashville, Richmond—but also of near-identical subjects. Well-dressed, well-groomed college kids, black and white, who sat at lunch counters. Except those photos weren't only of kids sitting. They were of something else, something more. And Molly felt fear, like something squeezing her esophagus, for she knew what was coming.

"We don't—don't serve Negroes here," Peggy the waitress said to the first young man, and one of the reporter's camera flashes froze her darting-eye uncertainty. "Whites only."

The young man in the gold-rimmed glasses said, "I'd like a cup of coffee please."

"Hey, Sambo, didn't you hear the lady? You ain't gonna get served here!" someone called out from the diner, and there was nervous but genuine laughter.

The young man blinked and said again, "I would like a cup of coffee please."

"Yeah, ain't this a diner?" the young woman in the flapper clothes said, and there was no trace of hesitancy in her voice. "You run out of coffee or something?"

The middle-aged blond man beside the young woman reached out and lightly patted her hand, and she turned to him, nodded, and quieted down. *So he's a part of the group*, Molly thought, still standing there, starting to feel like an idiot for not knowing where to go.

The doors from the kitchen opened, and Old Man Stoddard, the diner's owner, stepped out. His black BB eyes, shrunken by horn-rimmed glasses so thick, they looked like collapsible binoculars, seemed to grow even smaller with each step as he marched forward.

"You heard Peggy," Old Man Stoddard called to the group. "Don't wanna call the police on you people so why don't you—"

"Call the police?" the young woman said. "For what? Ordering coffee?"

"For trespassing on my property 'cause I don't want none of you here!"

By now, the audience of the diner was no longer quiet. There were shouts of "That's right," "You goddamn Yankees," and "This is his place!"

Molly heard the scrape of chairs being pulled back, and she turned to see the five young men who'd once been in her 9th-grade class from hell head toward the counter. Tall and marble-armed, the men bore little resemblance to their grasshopper-with-pimples teenage selves. All except their leader, a pint-sized greaser who, with his duck-butt haircut and red leather jacket, tried so hard to look like James Dean, he should've been sued for copyright infringement.

Stevie, Molly thought, recalling his name. *Stevie Suggs.* The little punk had stayed the same, right down to his insufferable smirk, which didn't waver even when he sipped from the large glass of lemonade he held.

"Hey, hey," Old Man Stoddard said to the advancing men. "Don't want no trouble."

"This ain't trouble. This is the top of the roller coaster." Stevie laughed and, stepping up to the counter, slapped the young black man on the back. "Hey, boy, didn't you hear the old man? Get your ass off that stool and scram."

The young black man said nothing, didn't even turn around. But he had begun to quietly shake, and Molly felt his fear on her like a cold, acrid wind, almost making her shiver herself. Stevie must've sensed something similar for his smirk widened, and, after seeing Molly standing there, even winked at her. Then he turned back to the black man.

"Guess you didn't hear me too good, did you? Your ears must be plugged or something. Here, let me clean them out for you."

Stevie chucked his glass of lemonade into the man's face, the splash of yellow liquid highlighted by several camera flashes. The young black man flinched, and the diner cheered, actually cheered at this. Molly put an open hand to her mouth, stricken with shock, but then, why should she be shocked? These exact moments had long been foreshadowed by the newspaper stories she'd been reading every other day.

"I'd like a cup of coffee please," the young black man said again.

Peggy the waitress stared at his rivulet-streaked face, and Molly observed three emotions navigate across her face at once—disbelief, anger, and a hint of admiration. She turned to Old Man Stoddard for help, but he only stared back with the same beseeching gape.

"Go—go call Hollis," Old Man Stoddard finally said. "Right now."

Peggy hurried back to the kitchen, presumably to where the phone was. As she disappeared through the double doors, she passed Cash, who came out holding a large frying pan. The sight, under any other circumstance, would've looked almost comical, except Molly saw that his face was beet red and the fingers wrapped around the handle were tense. She knew how strong he was, and though she didn't know what he was planning to do, as he turned toward the young black man, she fixed Cash with her sternest schoolmarm glare and mouthed, "Go back inside."

The boy didn't seem to get the message for an instant. Then he blinked twice, as if awakening from a trance. Under Molly's continued stare, he retreated back inside the kitchen.

She let out a sigh, but her relief didn't last because she returned her eyes to the lunch counter only to see Stevie holding another glass of what looked like Coca-Cola.

"Damn, boy, you really ain't budging from that seat," Stevie said to the drenched young man. "Guess that last splash didn't clear out your ears enough. You're one dirty Sambo, you know that?" His hangers-on giggled as if on cue, and Stevie pulled back his glass to chuck it again, accompanied by more hoots and laughter from the diner.

But the liquid never left the glass for the young woman in the flapper clothes whirled toward Stevie and said, "Not as dirty as you, boy. Next time, use soap made from pig lard, okay? Not pig shit."

Stevie blinked at this, his hand holding the glass frozen in place. Molly had recently seen the movie *Sayonara*, and it looked as if an invisible geisha artist had been at work, Stevie's face having turned so suddenly white. Molly would've bet her life's savings that he had never been addressed like this by a colored person before, much less an undersized girl who looked barely out of her teens. But then Stevie recovered, and the smirk was back in place, if haphazardly.

"You're one of them northern Negroes, ain't you? See, colored girls around here don't pop off like that. They're a lot sweeter. Let me give you some of that sweetness you're missing."

Stevie turned and spotted what he was looking for. He set his Coca-Cola glass down on the table at a nearby booth where a family was eating. He reached for a dish of half-eaten banana split. "Mind if borrow this?"

The burly, denim-wearing father said, "Go right ahead," and even smiled.

No, not smiled, Molly thought, sick to her stomach. Grinned. The man *grinned*.

And he wasn't the only one enjoying the spectacle. Behind her, Molly could hear more laughter and encouragement—"Drench her," "Do it," "Go for it!"—and she didn't want to turn to see who these people were for she already knew. Her neighbors, her colleagues, her friends.

Molly stood there paralyzed by what she was observing, more so because nobody came to the young woman's aid. Not the reporters and definitely none of the diner's patrons. Not even the middle-aged blond man, who just sat stoically on his stool, as unruffled as a yogi meditating. The man who was obviously part of the group and who had earlier ... what? Mesmerized Molly? She almost guffawed at the thought, so ridiculous was it in light of the current ugliness. No, the man seemed as passive as everyone else.

Except he wasn't. Unbidden came a strange thought, seemingly divorced from evidence, but it was there. With his longish blond hair and bulky body, the man appeared like a lion protecting his pride. But, if that were so, he sure had observed the injustice unfurling before him with a too-easy detachment, and Molly wondered why he didn't do something.

Why don't you? a small voice inside her asked. She had no answer. The whole weight of the room—her townsfolk, her upbringing— seemed to crush any initiative on her part. She'd never thought of herself as a coward, but she'd also never thought herself brave. And to risk her standing in town, to indeed risk everything, to help out a few "outside agitators" seemed too much to ask.

Yet, when Stevie said, "Here, honey," and prepared to shove the dish of banana split into the young woman's face, something in Molly broke.

"Put that down," Molly said, and in the resultant quiet of the diner, she could only hear her heartbeats, like a train speeding over track ties spaced just an inch apart.

Stevie turned to her. "What?"

"You heard me. You leave those kids alone, Stevie."

Her former student said nothing for an instant, then he laughed. "Where you think you're at, Miss Vail?" He'd spat out her name. "Your classroom? If you haven't noticed, I ain't a kid no more. So why don't you shut your pie hole?"

He turned away and went to throw the banana split again when Molly, before she was even aware of it herself, grabbed his wrist. The reaction was immediate and violent as Stevie yanked it away from her, the dish tumbling out of his hand and shattering on the floor. And—she heard gasps behind her—he raised that now unencumbered hand, the fingers curling into a fist.

Molly wasn't sure if he intended to strike her, and she didn't have time to flinch. And she would never know, for Stevie's wrist was abruptly encircled by one big hand, in precisely the same location where she had grabbed earlier. Except this new hand was so much larger than hers, and when Stevie yanked his arm like before, nothing moved.

She stepped back and followed the hand to the bowling-pin forearm attached to the bowling-ball bicep of the blond man, who had gotten off his stool and was regarding Stevie coolly.

So I was right, Molly thought in wonder. *He isn't passive, after all.*

"Now, I don't mind if you just—" the blond man began, but then Stevie gave another violent jerk with his arm, which moved approximately an inch or so before he cried out in alarm. "You listen, understand? Or I'm gonna snap your wrist like a twig."

Stevie, saucer-eyed, his other arm gripping the forearm the blond man held, nodded. His underlings looked bewildered and, like all bullies, were frozen in their indecision. The whole diner indeed seemed to watch with a mixture of shock and incredulity, even Stevie's erstwhile victim. Although, in the young flapper's case, that incredulity didn't preclude her from smiling a very wide, triumphant smile.

"As I was saying," the blond man said, eyeing an increasingly sweat-soaked Stevie, "I don't mind you pouring lemonade or whatever on us, but as soon as you hit a woman, I get mad. And that's one show you don't want the curtains to go up on."

Then, with apparently no effort, the blond man twisted his arm. Stevie yelped and, as if there were no intermediate steps, at once found himself on the floor, cradling his wrist with his other hand and making noises like a puppy whose tail had been stepped on.

The blond man, his face still rigid with anger, glanced away from this pathetic tableau, and as he did, his eyes met Molly's. At that moment, all the anger left his face, as if he'd been unplugged from a power source. He no longer looked like an avenging angel or even an overzealous Samaritan. He looked once again like what Molly suspected was his most natural self, a friendly man who'd sat next to her just a few minutes ago and asked what was good to eat. A friendly man who should never ever be pushed around.

But Molly didn't have time to dwell on this thought before she heard, from behind her, a familiar voice calling out, "Put all your hands behind your back!"

She turned to see Hollis heading into the diner with a half-dozen of the police department's blue-eyed boys. Each officer held handcuffs, and as they advanced toward the counter, each step was flashbulbed as if they were movie stars walking down a red carpet.

The blond man and everyone else at the lunch counter did as they were told and placed their hands behind their backs as Hollis and his men cuffed them.

"Hollis," Molly said, "they weren't doing anything except—"

"Molly, you should've knowed better," Hollis said, shackling the blond man, not meeting her eyes. "Helping them out like that."

Helping them out? She realized her childhood friend must've been right outside the diner, just looking in through the windows and observing. And he hadn't stepped in until the situation had swung decisively to the protesters' advantage.

Molly said, "Hollis, then you know damn well they weren't—"

"They were disturbing the peace!"

He pulled on the cuffs, and the blond man came with him, not protesting, though Molly knew if he had wanted to, he could've put Hollis in the hospital. She knew this as surely as the sun would rise tomorrow in the east.

Hollis jerked the man's wrists again, and this time, something clattered onto the floor, but Molly paid it no attention as she watched Hollis, still not meeting her gaze, shove the blond man toward the exit, followed by his deputies, each with a protester in tow.

They walked through a dry thunderstorm of camera flashes and roars of approval and derision from the diner patrons. "See how you like the coffee in prison!" "Serves you Yankees right!" "Hope you got your get-out-of-jail card!" Through the windows, Molly saw the protesters being crammed into the police cruisers parked by the curb, and then, sirens blaring, the cars reversed and were gone.

When she returned her gaze to the diner interior, she noticed Stevie had already gotten to his feet. He was still rubbing his wrist, and his bloodshot eyes were trained squarely on hers. The rage was so manifest, it felt almost physical. Not quite a violent shove but the anticipatory dread *before* the shove. As she glanced around, she felt the same anger, in varying degrees, from the diner's other patrons now that the object of their loathing was gone.

Even Cash, who had come out from the kitchen again, stared at her with … what? Not rage but disbelief, disapproval, and a repertoire of negative, even conflicting emotions that no sixteen-year-old face was up to expressing. Her one ally—her student, the oversized teenager, the very definition of a gentle giant—was gone.

Molly knew then that her life would never be the same, and as she prepared to leave the diner, she inadvertently stepped on something hard and wobbly on the floor. She looked down and realized it was what had slipped from the blond man's wrist when he had been handcuffed. She quickly reached down and picked it up then briskly walked out.

As she stepped outside, she felt the warmth of the sun on her face—and the even greater heat of her townsfolks' glares on her back.

CHAPTER 4

MOLLY

The next morning, after she'd just reconnected the phone in her living room, it rang. Molly hesitated, braced herself, and picked up the receiver.

"Hello?"

"You ever pick up your phone, Molly? I tried to reach you all day yesterday!"

Molly sighed, relieved by the familiar voice. Sally Harper, Hollis's wife. Her friend, like Hollis, since grammar school. Molly could picture her perched atop her high kitchen stool, where Molly often found her when visiting. Sally needed to be elevated when addressing her oversized son, whom many people couldn't believe *was* her child. Short-limbed and marshmallow-bodied, Sally possessed only one hard, well-defined feature, the rolled bangs that protruded above her forehead like the brim of a furry cap.

"Sorry, Sally," Molly said, "I'd disconnected the phone."

"What on earth for?"

"Let's just say I received more than a few unsolicited phone calls lately, and they weren't ads from the A&P."

"From who? What did they say?"

"People I didn't know, but they all seemed to know me. Or, at least, they all called me by the same word. Or, I should say, the same *two* words. The second being 'lover,' if you know what I mean."

"Those animals," Sally said after a pause. "I know they got a right to blow off some steam, but they ain't got no right to say that to you!"

Molly didn't know what to say to that because they, whoever *they* were, did have a right to say that to her. Instead, she asked how Cash was doing, and Sally said her son was fine and thanked her for getting him out of harm's way at the diner.

"I guess I'm not going to pussyfoot around, Molly. You know the whole town's talking about you, right? One of their own throwing in her lot with those outside agitators."

"I'm not throwing in my lot with anyone."

"But that's what people been saying. And truth be told, they have a point. I mean, everything's nice and good around here so why change anything?"

Molly felt her grip tighten on the phone. "Sally, a young man should be able to order a coffee without someone threatening to embed a lemonade glass into his head, don't you think?"

"Molly, he's a …"

Sally trailed off, and Molly was glad she did. Molly didn't want to think what her friend was going to say or how long their friendship would've lasted had she said the word.

"I'm just very confused," Sally finally said in a tired voice.

"We all are, I think."

"I know one thing, though."

"What's that?"

"They respect you now," Sally said.

They respect you now, Molly mused.

Although what she and Sally had in common could be pinched by a girl's barrette, their discussion of respect was a reoccurring talk—or rather the lack of respect that they and, Molly suspected, just about every woman in town felt from the men.

Certainly, Molly had her share of disregard in the classroom, but it was also in the faculty lounge, where her suggestions would often be brushed away by male colleagues like dandruff from their shoulders. The faculty lounge, the curbside police stop ("Driving a little fast there, missy"), the dinner dates ("You've got a hearty appetite"), everywhere and ever-present, the only variable being the length of time between the insults, whether measured in minutes, hours, or days but the interval never as long as whole weeks or months. Insults and, as she aged, insulting indifference.

"Yup," Molly told Sally, "they respect me so much now, they're actually calling on their own dime to say, 'Fuck you, bitch.'"

The comment elicited first an intake of breath from her friend then a bewildered laugh.

"If any of those gentleman callers show up at your door," Sally said, "you call Hollis straight away, you hear? I won't lie. You ain't exactly at the top of his favorite people's list right now, but if you call, he'll come, sure as crap through a goose. So, don't you hesitate."

"I won't. But I doubt anyone's going to show up besides reporters."

"Reporters?"

"Yes, a few," Molly said, remembering the men, four in all, each one, in his too-big suit and Buddy Holly hornrims, looking like a mimeographed copy of the previous. More polite than the phone callers but no less invasive, their insistent door knocks punctuating requests delivered in unmistakably Yankee accents: "We'd like to discuss what happened at the diner."

No, she didn't want to discuss it, didn't even open the door, and took the business cards off the doorjamb and placed them in what she'd long ago designated the Forget About It drawer.

She didn't want to answer any questions because she didn't want to antagonize her hometown more than she already had. Besides, she didn't want to *answer* questions; she wanted *her* questions answered. Specifically, what had happened to the arrested protesters? What, truth be told, had happened to *him?*

After she'd said goodbye to Sally, Molly went to her front door and found her town's paper had already been delivered. The story was on the front page, pressed to the bottom third by the Kennedy-Khrushchev summit in Vienna, but still prominent. The headline simply read, "Sit-In at The Porky Pie," and she was glad it was written by Lloyd Renfro, the reporter most sympathetic to similar protests in the South. So sympathetic, Molly knew, his house was often picketed by people waving placards proclaiming him a communist.

In her kitchen, Molly read the article, and it didn't disappoint. Its description was pretty spot-on as to what had happened—the sit-in, the bullying, the arrest—and she felt as if she'd entered an invisible sauna as she recalled the injustice. But then her anger had to jostle with a rising panic as she read, "The bullying was interrupted by one of our town's own brave souls—Molly Valle, an English teacher at South High School—who stopped the flinging of a chocolate cake into the face of one of the young protesters."

It was a banana split, Molly mentally corrected, ever the schoolteacher. As she put down the paper, she thought, *Brave soul*, and almost laughed. The bravest action she felt she had ever taken was handling those intervention English classes and divorcing her husband a decade earlier, this latter action praised by her friends with a mixture of a quarter admiration and three-quarters pity. Brave to be alone.

As she picked up the paper and continued reading, all these mental meanderings terminated as she came across two sentences: "The arrested protesters spent the night in jail but were released this morning. Their sit-in demonstrations, funded by the Congress of Racial Equality and coordinated by one John Pressman of New York, are expected to continue this week from their headquarters at Jupiter Hammon College."

John.

Molly matched the face with the name. A simple name, a common name, but a strong one too. A no-nonsense name. One that matched the blond man at the lunch counter. How she knew this, she wasn't sure. But she did know one thing: he was at Jupiter Hammon College. A historically black college just outside the city limits, a location she'd driven past innumerable times on the highway. Not a ten-minute drive from where she sat at her kitchen table.

She put the paper down and looked across the tabletop to where the man's watch was lying—the item that had fallen from his wrist at The Porky Pie and she had picked up. She reached across and held it up in her hand like an archaeologist inspecting an unearthed artifact.

The watch lived up to expectations. An American watch—a Waltham with a white face, large black numbers, and an olive canvas band. Unremarkable so far but covering that unremarkable face was a brass grill like the visor of a medieval knight's helmet. A visor with a dozen eye holes, one for each hour. It was no doubt a military watch, a warrior's watch, and it suited the blond man as perfectly as his name. Except for one thing in his case: the brass grill shouldn't have been on the surface but beneath it. The power under the everyday surface.

Suddenly, Molly wanted very much to see the watch returned to the blond man's wrist. To *John Pressman's* wrist. That thick, sun-browned wrist that had prevented her from being struck by one of her former students.

Yes, his watch needed to be returned, and immediately after that thought, Molly spoke aloud in the still loneliness of her kitchen, "Are you crazy?"

CHAPTER 5

JOHN

Jupiter Hammon College, a traditionally black school, was named after an 18th-century enslaved poet and founded in 1871 by what locals then denigrated as "carpetbaggers." The cluster of five red-brick buildings was a ten-minute drive from downtown, very convenient for the city's students to get to but far enough so it wouldn't remind the white townsfolk of their loss in the War of Northern Aggression. The need for discretion was further heightened when, during the 1930s highway boom, a thirty-foot-wide ribbon of concrete passed not a hundred feet from its entrance, which necessitated a wall of Leyland cypresses to obscure the college's presence from passing white motorists.

This privacy appealed to the Congress of Racial Equality, which made the college's summer-abandoned dorms the living quarters for its volunteers. A dozen wooden, bare-bones shoeboxes that resembled military barracks more than student housing—which, John Pressman decided, was just as well. They were, after all, in a low-intensity war of sorts with the town.

He sat in the white-walled common room of one of the dorms, freshly bathed but with an equally fresh layer of sweat in the heat. On the tabletop before him lay a disfigured, half-eaten sandwich. The sandwich with no taste or even smell, and to John, who had always been around food that had a scent—delicious, sweet, rancid, *something*—that fact was unfathomable.

"Listen," he said, "if we're still alive tomorrow morning after eating this, I promise to cook us a decent breakfast."

Bethanee Avery, sitting across the table and the only other person in the room, provided a small nod above the paper she was reading. No longer in her flapper clothes, she was dressed in a colorful dashiki, whose shapelessness didn't detract from her cool and collected self.

That she could stay cool in this heat was remarkable, John decided. That she was able to after the past two days' events was even more so. The arrest, the jail cells, the overnight stay, the morning arraignment, the bond, the release. The swarming of reporters at the courthouse, the interviews, and the drive back to Jupiter Hammon, only stopping along the way to pick up the sawdust-flavored sandwiches from a gas station, and, for the past hour or so, eating and poring over the newspapers for write-ups of the diner sit-in. After ascertaining the stories had been sympathetic and good, the scattering of everyone except John and Bethanee to their dorm rooms to make up for, in the late Mississippi afternoon, last night's lost sleep.

Except they both had company as William appeared, dressed in grandpa-hoary pajamas. He nodded to them, went to the icebox near the corner, and took out the jar of milk. As he poured himself a glassful, he said, "Couldn't sleep. Maybe this will help."

John studied the young man and saw he didn't look as tired or as defeated as at the diner. He looked like himself again, the proper dentist's son he'd always been, but John wondered how much effort it took for him to hold everything in.

"Just make sure you get your forty winks tonight," Bethanee told William, "'cause tomorrow we're gonna get our forty lashes."

John grimaced along with William. True, there were more sit-ins planned tomorrow and, just as likely, more humiliation and possible arrests. But hardly lashes.

"I will," the young man replied, and John noticed again how he never looked Bethanee squarely in the face. "Good evening," William said and, with a quick sheepish glance at Bethanee, took his glass of milk and disappeared down the hall. When John turned back to Bethanee, he wasn't surprised to see the slight upcurve of her lips.

"I know," she told John, even before he could ask the question. Then, changing topics, she asked, "The press has been good, right?" And she nodded toward the newspapers.

"Yes."

The angle steepened on those upcurved lips. "But it could've been better, right?"

"Yes, it could've been better," John said and knew what she was smiling about.

He had, after all, violated the basic tenet of passive resistance: don't retaliate. The Congress of Racial Equality had drummed this lesson into all of its volunteers and answered any skepticism by pointing out that Gandhi had brought down the British Empire with passive resistance. The philosophy was simple: your suffering, when documented by newspaper accounts, particularly photos, would advance your cause far more than if you tried to momentarily end that torment by striking back.

But while John intellectually understood the tenet, he had never fully accepted it. His whole being—his upbringing, his life experience—rebelled against it. He'd read Ralph Waldo Emerson's "Self-Reliance" in high school and had never forgotten its central doctrine: "No law can be sacred to me but that of my nature ... The only right is what is after my constitution, the only wrong what is against it." Those words always rang true to him, which was why he couldn't stand by and let some punk strike a woman, even knowing that allowing her to be hit—he could imagine the headline: "Segregationist Hits White Woman!"—would've presented a public-relations coup for the protesters.

"Didn't think you had it in you, John," Bethanee said, still grinning. "Made me shake all over, like a leaf."

"You know that's not true. Nothing scares you."

"Oh, you did. The way you handled that cracker. Rescuing your damsel in distress."

"Who?" John said, but he knew he was fooling no one. The woman the "cracker" was going to hit—her face had been on the periphery of all his conscious thoughts since yesterday. And now he had a name, courtesy of newspaper accounts. "The bullying was interrupted by one of our town's own brave souls—Molly Valle, an English teacher at South High School ..." Molly Valle. *Valle*—a name unique for these parts, he'd guess. A name more common where he'd grown up, in the Lower East Side of New York City.

"Who?" Bethanee chuckled. "I guess she's attractive in a school-marm kind of way. Those glasses. But she's a bit ... old, don't you think?"

"If you haven't noticed, Bethanee, *I'm* old."

"You don't seem too old to me." She held his gaze, and this time, her expression wasn't one of bratty amusement.

Is this really happening again? John wondered. What he knew about women could fit beneath a seashell at Coney Island, but he had formed a few postulates in regard to the opposite gender. Postulate number one: Treat every woman with respect. Postulate two: You don't need to have sex with every woman you meet. Ergo, postulate three: Since you don't need to have sex with every woman you meet, why not just be yourself with all women?

Sure, these ideas were not as assured as Emerson's pronouncements, but they had served John well through the years. Although, by following all three consistently, he had sometimes encountered a strange phenomenon: women you'd least expect to find *you* attractive do.

Like the intelligent, beautiful woman sitting across from him. Except she wasn't even a woman but a girl. At least, that was how he saw her. A girl nearly thirty years younger than he was. Thirty much too young years.

"I guess that's that," John said, not even sure what that meant. He stood up. "We got to get up early tomorrow, and I know it's a bit early but ..." He looked down at his watch and spotted the white band of skin around his browned wrist.

"Did you lose your watch?" Bethanee asked, missing nothing.

John nodded. "Maybe back at the diner, maybe somewhere else. I don't remember."

"Was it valuable?"

John began to shake his head, reconsidered, then nodded. "It was just a cheap wristwatch, hardly worth anything. But it belonged to my father. And, well, it was his." Saying the words made him feel sad, and he felt the loss like watching a precious artifact disappear into the depths of a bottomless ocean. "Well, good evening, Bethanee."

He began heading to the back of the building, where his dorm room was.

"John."

He stopped and turned to Bethanee, who was still sitting and eyeballing him.

"I've got an extra watch," she told him. "I can bring it to you later tonight. I think you'll be impressed by how precisely its hands move."

So, there it is, John thought in amazement, out in the open, with no camouflage. A part of him was undeniably flattered. Fifty years old, with no money or great looks (he thought so anyway), and this young, striking girl wanted him, if only for a night. A lot of fellows his age would've loved to be standing where he was, and he knew of several marriages that had been decimated by the choices such men made.

But here was the thing about chasing youth: even if you finally captured it, the hands holding on would remain thick-veined, middle-aged hands. The relationship, if one could even call it that, would be nothing but a fantasy, a chimera, and though John didn't lack imagination, he always wanted to be in reality when it came to women. And the first step in being in a reality-based relationship with a woman was finding a *woman* and not a girl.

So he found himself saying, "I'm flattered, Bethanee, but I think I'm too old to appreciate such movements." Before the girl could formulate a decent retort, John turned and fled down the hall.

Ten minutes later, after brushing his teeth and washing his face, John was back in his room at the back of the dorm. The building's military-barracks exterior extended to its no-frills interior, and so he hung up his shirt on a plain clothes rack and put his pants in a rust-speckled footlocker. A couple more pairs of pants and a few more shirts—all the clothes he owned.

In fact, the twelve-by-twelve-foot room contained everything he owned. His clothes, assorted pens and notebooks, and several books—cookbooks, Emerson, Thoreau's *Walden*, among others. He had some cash in the bank, but that had been steadily drying up since he had, against the advice of all his friends, quit his "real" job and gone into civil rights full time. With the loss of a bonafide *paying* job had come the loss of all the accouterments that his previous, relatively well-to-do lifestyle had allowed. The spacious apartment in Greenwich Village, the V8-powered Chevrolet coupe, the disposable income that had allowed him vacations to Canada and the Florida Keys.

But he had gained something most people lacked: a purpose in life. As John lay down, closed his eyes, and began to drift off to sleep, he thought how, five years previously, he had realized that the only way to happiness was through a life of helping others. What he hadn't counted on, though, was how exciting such a life could be. Beneath the reason of helping people, beneath all the altruism, he had to admit that undeniably selfish part of him.

"I'm on a great adventure," he muttered to himself, and though he looked forward to his sleep, he knew he would bound up once he awakened. And possibly see that teacher again. Molly Valle. *Valle* …

Just when he was about to cross the border between consciousness and unconsciousness, there was a knock at the door. He opened his eyes and saw Bethanee poking her head in. *This isn't funny anymore*, he thought, intending to make his refusal far firmer this time.

But before he could say anything, Bethanee said, "You have a visitor."

"What? Who?"

"Your damsel. The schoolmarm."

"What?"

Bethanee flashed a crescent of teeth. "She's right outside," she said and closed the door behind her.

John got out of bed—he didn't want to think he bolted out—his tiredness at once AWOL. As he dressed, he thought of a fourth postulate about women, one that encompassed not only young men or old men but every man between puberty and death. From all corners of the world, from all eras, from Neanderthal man to Renaissance man:

When you're attracted to a woman, just about everything else goes out the window.

CHAPTER 6

MOLLY

On a late-June afternoon in 1961, John Lennon and Paul McCartney were unknown musicians playing in a Hamburg music club, the price of a gallon of gasoline was twenty-seven cents, and Molly Valle was waiting in the common room of a college dormitory.

She sat primly on an uncomfortable high-back chair, her hands in her lap. She thought she looked like a schoolgirl out on her first date. The only thing missing was a bouquet of flowers. But her rigid sitting posture was by design. If she'd stood, she wasn't sure she wouldn't start swaying—or if her beating heart wouldn't propel her this way or that, as if she'd swallowed a live animal that was trying to get out.

It had been ten minutes since she'd driven off the highway to Jupiter Hammon College, and she'd taken the drive only after a couple of hours of deliberation. Driving up to the small parking lot, the hot air redolent of the surrounding brush. She had parked and then just sat there, eyeing the red-brick dormitory where she guessed the protesters would be, her body enveloped by the heat, which the forthcoming evening didn't alleviate. It wasn't only a matter of meeting someone, even someone she found attractive.

No, she was meeting what the town would consider the enemy, crossing to the other side. So she'd sat there, five long minutes in her white summer dress with the red-apple prints—*why the hell did I pick this one?*—and sweated it out. Then her left hand, as if by itself, opened the door, and her legs, apparently without guidance, propelled the rest of her out of the car.

Five minutes after she'd walked in and asked the only person in the common room if "Mr. Pressman" was in. It was, of course, the same young woman from the diner. She was no longer wearing her flapper sailor outfit but a colorful, African-looking dress, looking as regal as an Ashanti princess surveying her realm—if such a person possessed no sweat pores, since the girl looked as cool as if it were snowing outside. And she no longer sported a scowl but a smile—a knowing and not altogether friendly smile. She didn't seem the least bit surprised to find the white woman from the diner in front of her again.

"I'll go find Mr. Pressman," she said, stressing the "Pressman." When she disappeared down the hallway, that deliberate smile never left her face.

As Molly waited, the unreality of her situation hit her again. The change from yesterday was too wide. A day ago, she was tutoring the son of the police chief. A day ago, she was still a respectable—*but were you really?* a small voice asked—member of the community. A day ago, she hadn't been one of the town's most despised citizens.

A day ago, I wouldn't have been here.

Except a day ago, she wasn't the same person. A day ago, at the diner, she had been issued an invisible passport and had been transported to this world. A world that looked exactly like her old world but which was different in fundamental, unalterable ways. What was that recent show with the handsome young narrator? *The Twilight Zone*—yes, that was what it was.

Yet, despite her discomfort, the woman with the invisible passport wanted to be here. For here, at last, was a break from the stultifying routine that had been her life for so, so long. She wasn't quite living the life of quiet desperation so famously described by Henry Thoreau, but it was close. Too damned close.

She had her students and her job and her house, and, while she liked all three, life had become a roulette wheel where the spinning ball never quite descended. Just an endless spin that coincided with the hours of the day. But now, the roulette wheel had spiraled off its axis, the ball catapulted upward, and both had gone tumbling down the carpet and out of the casino altogether.

But Molly had no time to savor that image when the girl emerged from the hallway, and, moments later, John Pressman entered the room.

"Hi, you were looking for me?" He was smiling like the young woman. His smile, though, was open and curious, without the least bit of sardonic amusement.

"Hello, Mr. Pressman." Molly was pleased to find her voice steady.

She stood up. "I'm not sure if you remember me." Immediately, she felt silly with that remark.

Of course, he remembers you.

In the caressing orange of the through-the-window, late-afternoon sunshine, however, Molly wasn't so sure. Her hair was different, and she was no longer wearing the blue dress at the diner. She knew she looked different, as only people between the first and second impressions could look different. But a startling realization overpowered these ruminations. John Pressman didn't look the same either.

Away from the frenzy at the diner, she could see him more clearly. He looked smaller, though still substantial with wide, muscular shoulders and, courtesy of the white T-shirt he was wearing, thick arms. Large fellow, no doubt, but no longer gladiator-sized. The same over-long blond hair was there, but Molly could now see the temples were gray. A flint spark of a worry: *Is he older or younger than me?* A couple of years older, Molly decided, noting the wrinkles on the man's face, wrinkles the slanting light accentuated. Dressed in his simple shirt and blue jeans, he looked like any other man.

Except, he didn't. Not really. And she guessed the main reason was *how* he looked at her. His gaze contained none of the attributes she'd become accustomed to from men after she'd turned forty: indifference, dismissiveness, even disdain. Instead, he looked at her with … admiration? Yes, admiration—Molly was sure of it. And though he was a stranger, he didn't seem like one. He seemed like an old friend you hadn't seen in a while and who, emerging from a taxi, you noticed had changed his hairstyle or wardrobe. The look of *superficial* difference.

"I remember you," the man with the open, admiring gaze said. "How could I forget? Besides, you're all over the papers, Molly Valle."

"Yes," she said and smiled. "I wish that weren't so, but …" She stopped.

Molly Valle, he had said. VALLE—*VI YAY*. The correct way—the Spanish-language way. Not "Molly *Vail*"—which was what she'd been called all her life. Until this moment, in 1961, by a stranger who didn't seem like a stranger but a friend.

"Can I get you something, Bethanee?" John suddenly said and turned to the young woman behind him. The girl had been bouncing her eyes between him and Molly like a spectator at Wimbledon. Now, she snapped out of her trance and even blinked.

"Nope," Bethanee said and, after a recalcitrant moment, took the hint and began to retreat to the hallway. But before departing, she added a tart, "You two have fun now."

"A real spitfire," John said when the girl was finally gone.

"I know the type." Molly thought of all the smart, mouthy girls she'd taught over the years, their only difference from Bethanee being their age and complexion.

"Like a seat?" John offered, and Molly nodded. Together they sat at the center table, which was festooned with newspapers. "Bit of a mess, I'm afraid. Would you like something to drink?"

Molly shook her head. "I came here to thank you, Mr. Pressman."

"Thank me?"

"The diner. For preventing my former student from hitting me."

"Oh that." John made a wave with his hand, as if preventing a case of assault were no more onerous than opening a stuck window. "I should be thanking you for that."

"Me? For what?"

"For taking a stand. Trust me, it's a rarity."

"Is that right?" Despite herself, she enjoyed the compliment.

"Are you okay?"

"I'm fine, though I should be asking you that question. How's your other colleague? That young man."

"William? He's fine. Nothing a long night's sleep couldn't cure."

Molly nodded and was about to ask how Hollis had treated them. But she stopped herself. Did John Pressman really need to know that she was childhood friends with the chief of police, who used to copy her algebra homework in the ninth grade? No, he didn't need to know that.

So she simply smiled, and John smiled back. Molly wondered how long they'd keep smiling at each other. But the uncomfortable silence didn't materialize. He not only looked like a long-lost friend but felt like one too, as if they were both roasting marshmallows over a campfire.

Finally, she said to him, "But I didn't only come here to thank you." *I came here to see you*—the words on the tip of her tongue. "I also brought this."

She reached into her purse and withdrew the watch she'd recovered from the diner floor. His eyes went to the watch and widened in elated surprise. But then they returned to her face, as if, having been presented with something beautiful, his eyes decided the former view was still better. Molly, who hadn't been on the receiving end of such appreciation in a long, long time, grew flustered and almost dropped the watch when she handed it over.

"Thank you so much." John wrapped the watch around the pale, untanned strip on his wrist. "You have no idea how pleased I am to have this again."

"It's definitely a distinctive watch." Molly nodded toward the grill that covered its face. "Like it's going off to war. Did it come with a miniature armored horse?"

John laughed. "No, but you're not far off. It's a World War One trench watch. The grill's called, if I remember right, a shrapnel guard. My old man, only a few years after stepping off the boat from Odessa, joined the US Army and was issued this. This has traveled to France and back."

Molly could imagine the watch in France, in rat-choked trenches and across bullet-punched battlefields. Could imagine it surviving the Meuse-Argonne Offensive where American Doughboys helped win the war under limb-ripping, cordite-suffused bombardments. Could see it being worn on the thin, mud-encrusted wrist of an underfed young man, John Pressman's father, forty-plus years in the past. The immigrant father from Odessa—the seaport in Ukraine, wasn't it? Yes, Molly was sure of it. But how to reconcile that samovar-and-borscht landscape with the decidedly WASPy surname of Pressman?

These questions, however, became submerged by a more pressing one: how long could she sit like this before her presence became abnormal? She had come to thank him. She had returned his watch.

Now what? Was this the end then? If not of their friendship but of something *beyond* friendship? Was this one of those moments she'd had when the possibility of a potentially spellbinding moment in life was dashed by cold reality? It had happened before, countless times before, and it would happen again.

In the distant future, when looking back, she would think how silly it had been for her to think that at forty-eight years of age she could just meet a stranger and somehow, following the proverbial finger snap, her life would change. The naiveté of it, the infantilism of it. As if, having taught teenagers for so long, she had reverted to being one herself, with an equally callow understanding of how the world worked. The realm of Bogart-Bacall movies and Shakespearean sonnets that adults always outgrew for they knew it … was … not … reality.

But then John asked, "Say, you wanna get something to eat? You hungry?"

"No," Molly's stomach said. "Yes," her lips said.

CHAPTER 7

JOHN

So, there he was at another diner. If The Porky Pie downtown could be called a greasy spoon, this place—he didn't catch the name upon entering—was *the* greasy spoon, and a delectable one at that.

John Pressman loved the place. Loved how the blinds sliced the late-afternoon sunlight, stenciling the room into alternating bars of gold and black. Loved how the air itself was heavy with oily yet savory smells, as if he'd dunked his head into a deep fryer—minus the death-inducing high temperature, of course. He even loved the clientele: burly men in flannel shirts and with five o'clock shadows—interstate truckers from the nearby highway and amazingly multi-ethnic due to *this* diner's nonexistent whites-only policy.

This last point was the reason he guessed she'd had him drive here, the place being far from downtown and its prying, judging eyes. Molly Valle, who sat and smiled at him from across the worn linoleum table.

"That boy from the kitchen," John said, remembering the hulking teenager in the kitchen doorway back at The Porky Pie. "You know him, right?"

"Cash Harper was—*is*—one of my students at school. I tutor him during the summers."

"Harper. Wait, he's the son of the police chief?"

"One and the same. Everybody's connected one way or another in this town."

"You did him a good turn at the diner," John said. "Telling him to go back inside. I mean, I didn't think that was possible with just a nod of your head."

"He's … afraid of me. Don't let his size fool you. Inside, he's a golden retriever puppy, though everyone wants him to be an adult pit bull."

"Why's that?"

"To be more aggressive. His father wants him to excel at football, which I guess you'd need a certain aggressiveness to do well in. The thing is, though, he's not good at football, but he's dazzling at math. He wants to be an engineer, and if he just tunes out what his family and friends tell him, he just might become one and live happily ever after."

Their meal arrived—a cheeseburger for him, an egg-salad sandwich for her—delivered by the blond waitress with the pinched face, as if taking their orders earlier had been akin to sucking on a lemon.

They watched her go, and when Molly turned her face back to him, John could see a suppressed chuckle wobbling her lips.

He took a bite of his cheeseburger to stifle his own laugh and asked, "So what makes you so different?"

"Am I different?"

"You are, and I think everybody thinks so too."

She smiled at this but said nothing. They ate in silence for a moment, just two ordinary people enjoying an ordinary meal. But John knew it was no ordinary meal for the simple reason that Molly Valle was no ordinary woman.

How many people could've done what she did at the diner?

Not many, he guessed. Not only would most folks have lacked the courage to do so but, more importantly, lacked the intelligence and honesty to see the ugly racial reality of their town. Most people indeed never fully saw reality in most situations in life. They lacked the ability to perceive what Aristotle had famously described as seeing A for A, the law of identity's "whatever is, is." Or, to use George Orwell's more recent construction, "To see what is in front of one's nose needs a constant struggle"—a struggle that most people failed at. But not Molly Valle. She saw right past the gray, man-constructed walls and roofs of her town and perceived the green grassland beyond and cerulean skies above.

My God, he thought, *what intelligence*. What incandescent, penetrating intelligence.

"I guess I do feel different," she said as she finished her sandwich. "Ever since I was a little girl. But I certainly haven't lived my life differently from any of my friends. College, a regular job, errands on the weekends. Just a normal life like everybody else. So how different could I have really been?"

"The hobgoblin of consistency," John said, thinking of Emerson again.

Molly nodded, and to John, she looked exactly like the school teacher she was, albeit a very glamorous one. "That's right. Few of us can go against the grain."

"You did."

"I'm not sure about that if you take my life as a whole," she said. "And thanks for not asking me if I've heard of 'Self Reliance.'"

"Why would I ask that? You're an English teacher."

"Oh, you'll be surprised by how much—or I should say, how little—people think of what you know. Even among colleagues I've known for decades."

"Your male colleagues, you mean."

"That's right. My male colleagues," Molly said and looked at him in a peculiar way, as if she couldn't quite believe a man was agreeing with her about other men.

But John never felt the insecurity that underlay the surfaces of most men, and in his mind, he could easily conjure up those male colleagues of hers. In the teachers' lounge, in their stiff suits with their bow-tied collars, their nicotine-yellowed fingers holding up their pretentious pipes, eyeing Molly as she came in, then snickering when she went out, dismissing her not because she didn't know enough but because she knew *too* much, indeed knew far more than they did, and they were cognizant of and frightened by this fact. Hence, the dismissal and, concomitantly, the figurative puffing out of their chests, like those of exotic birds whose impressive plumage hid the scrawny bodies beneath.

The waitress came by and cleared the table, and then a question issued from her pinched mouth that sounded like if they wanted dessert or not. John offered to split a slice of chocolate cake with Molly, and she said yes.

"You're different, Mr. Pressman," Molly said once the waitress had gone. "You're the first person in four decades who's called me by my real name."

"Valle, right? I knew those two years of high school Spanish would come in handy. So how does a nice Southern belle have that last name?"

"My grandfather was Mexican. Folks around here compliment me on how easily I get tanned during the summers, but really nobody knows about my background because I've been Molly *Vail* since the second grade."

"What happened then?" John asked, trying not to dwell on Molly's tan.

"My teacher, Mr. Robertson, went through the roster on the first day of school, and when he pronounced my last name as 'Vail,' I told him it was 'VI-YAY.' But he scrunched up his face and said, 'Where do you get VI from a V and an A? And where do you get a Y from two L's? No, little girl, you're gonna be called Molly Vail, and that's it.' And I've been Molly Vail ever since."

John and Molly shared a laugh, and when the cake arrived, they ate and talked about their families. Her father, who had died a decade earlier, and her mother remarrying and living in Florida. Her brother, Art, who moved to Hollywood to become an actor—"I'm going to be the next Anthony Quinn!" were his parting words when he left home—but ended up owning an air-conditioning business instead. John, in turn, told her about his family. Both parents passed away and two sisters alive and well in New York City—one a nurse in Brooklyn and the other a housewife in Queens.

"And you left everything behind," Molly said, and John detected a small note of amazement in her voice. "To come here to Mississippi."

"Wasn't particularly hard to do. Never married, no kids, not even a mortgage. It was easy to change my mind fast. A lot of people, including my own sisters, didn't understand me at all, though."

"'Is it so bad, then, to be misunderstood?'" Molly said.

John smiled. Emerson and "Self-Reliance" again. "Not one bit. Being misunderstood gave me a purpose in life and also this grand adventure I'm currently on."

"Is that so?" she asked, and he observed the amusement in both her eyes and lips. "In this fine establishment we find ourselves in?"

"Especially here," John said.

Which was true enough, and it was all due to the woman in front of him. He looked across the greasy spoon and was once again surprised that not every pair of male eyes was directed at her—or, in an even more appropriate response, the men becoming bug-eyed and salivating like the Warner Bros. cartoon wolf. Were other men blind? Stupid? Or, like men everywhere, were the diner's customers so conditioned by billboards, by magazines, and by television to only appreciate women whom society deemed attractive?

Yes, John thought, *the last case is likely the most plausible one.*

He had grown up in New York City and had often worked in fields surrounded by women whom society adored and revered. The slim, the young … the interchangeable, the undernourished. The women showcased in advertisements and commercials and on TV shows. Women he never really considered interesting or attractive. To him, they were breathing mannequins displaying accouterments. Makeup, form-fitting clothes, handbags, whatever, which were all very fetching, true, but accouterments all the same. They only decorated the shell of a person but never her soul. And without individualizing a woman, without seeing her soul, there was no real glamour.

In Molly, however, there was real glamour. He could sense it and even measure it, the quality being quantifiable like units on a scale—except, in her case, her allure was overflowing the pan. Society valued young, often blank women, but John never understood why this was the case. It was akin to going to a museum and being happy to gaze at perfectly white canvases.

To some men, maybe even to most men—the insecure, the easily manipulated men, most of male humanity really—that might be exciting. They could impress on the blank women their own personality and needs and wants. But that held no appeal whatsoever with John. He didn't go to a museum to draw or to change masterpieces to his own liking. He went there to appreciate the masterpieces in their own right.

And Molly was indeed a masterpiece, her face an exquisite painting, and he wished so much to get to know all the brushstrokes that had formed that portrait. What sad events deepened the furrows on her forehead? What scenes of happiness had etched those laugh lines on the edges of her mouth and eyes? What outside hobbies had caused her face and arms to glow golden brown? What had she been doing when she'd purchased that dress, those earrings, that lipstick? An infinite number of small details that John could spend a lifetime to study.

Men and women had been bamboozled. They had forgotten the first-hand enchantment that could exist between women and men and had instead settled for what second-hand experiences— advertisements and television—could bring. Such shallowness, such silliness, such willingness to be manipulated! So much so that, once again, John was stupefied that not every man in the diner had turned his head to Molly Valle.

They've missed out, he thought and felt a tremendous satisfaction. They had missed seeing below the surface of things—where the magic lay.

"So, you're telling me you're having a grand adventure every day now?" Molly asked.

"Not always," John admitted. "But I try to wake up every day thinking I am on one. And generally, reality is obliging. Especially today."

CHAPTER 8

MOLLY

Molly thought an after-dinner walk would be nice, to absorb the ten thousand calories she felt she'd just ingested. John agreed. After buying a couple beers from a liquor store next to the diner and getting a blanket from the trunk of his car, he followed her into the line of trees that served as a thick green curtain between civilization and the river. The sounds of the cars on the highway soon became muted, like those of a low-volume radio heard through walls.

It was night, or at least it should've been night since it was past eight. But the Mississippi summer day was reluctant to leave and pushed back the darkness, the sunlight intensifying into an over-strained orange. All that passed under the light appeared aware of this struggle between day and night. Flying insects excitedly buzzed by Molly's ear, and plants and even never-alive things—dirt, rocks, air itself—emitted their scents and odors at seemingly twofold strength. As she walked, she felt the dirt path's heat radiating through the thin soles of her sensible shoes.

She'd been on this path before, many times, but those walks had never felt like this. It was him. He made it, made everything, new. She felt him behind her, admiring her, and she smiled at her own conceit. When was the last time a man had admired her so? She didn't remember. Nor did she ever recall a man so self-assured as to completely trust her—or any woman—to know where she was going.

Yes, John Pressman, you are different.

And then they were there, passing the final zigzag of trees and brush, stepping onto a bluff overlooking the Mississippi River and the rolling lime hills beyond. She had seen this view before, but now, with her line of sight expanding from the few feet to the next tree to the countless miles to the far horizon, the vista hit her like a tangible force. The panorama was impossibly wide, and everything was so lit up by the amber rays of the still-defiant sun, the world seemed almost ethereal.

No, not ethereal, Molly thought as she closed her eyes. *Not ethereal but … primordial.* She smelled air unsullied by any trace of the mid-20th century—car exhaust, gasoline, laundry detergent—and she heard no revving engine or clanking dishes, only the sounds of the river, the insects, and the wind through the trees. With her eyes still closed, she suddenly could observe large scaly animals drink from the river, strange long-armed creatures hanging from trees, and fluttering dragonflies as big as pelicans. Startled, she opened her eyes, blinked, and tens, hundreds of millions of years flashed by, and she was in

1961 again. She saw the landscape wasn't primordial at all. Barges and tugboats glided languidly on the river, and the only large thing flying was an airliner high up in the sky.

Now, what was that? Molly turned to John and saw him smiling at her.

"Quite a sight, isn't it?" he said, and at that moment, she knew he knew what she'd just seen. How he knew, she wasn't sure. How *she* knew, she was even less sure. But there it was, a certainty that went beyond logic to the truth of the universe.

They spread out the blanket and had their beer picnic, an undertaking that Molly was surprised didn't cause a Mount Vesuvius to erupt inside her stuffed gut. Her stomach thankfully stayed calm, which allowed her to sit near but not too near John Pressman and just enjoy the moment, the silence so comfortable it could've come with its own bedding.

But her enjoyment couldn't compare with John's. Leaning back on one elbow and drinking from his beer, he looked like he should've been placed under the word "contentment" in an illustrated dictionary or on the book cover of James Joyce's never-written sequel, *A Portrait of the Artist as a Middle-Aged Man*. And that latter, nonsensical image caused Molly, sitting cross-legged a couple of feet away, to laugh out loud.

"What is it?" John asked, one eyebrow arched.

"I don't know. I guess I just never met anyone who enjoyed beer so much."

"It's not just the beer but the entire ambience of the place." He waved the bottle at the landscape. "Did you grow up around here?"

"Not too far from here actually. My parents' place, I mean, not where I'm at now. I used to come here with friends and play games."

John sat up and said, "Like what?"

Like what? Molly almost laughed. She had never met a man who was so curious about her, even of unimportant minutiae.

"The usual. Tag, hide-and-go-seek. Nothing too intellectual, I'm afraid. A lot of time, though, I'd just come here by myself. Bring a book to read and think deep, serious thoughts, like only kids can do. Thought about what I wanted to do with my life. Planned everything out."

Molly smiled, reminiscing. Her mind conjured up her too-serious, skinny-as-a-beanpole,   tanned-brown-by-the-Mississippi-summer twelve-year-old self. Then, with no apparent conscious thought, her forty-eight-year-old self added, "Not that any of those plans worked out or anything."

Even as she said those words, she wasn't sure why she'd said them. The statement, undeniably true though it was, seemed much too serious for the moment, even with the tacked-on, flippant "or anything." But while, by any rational standard, John Pressman was still a stranger, Molly felt she didn't want to hide anything from this man or pretend her life was everything she'd hoped for. All her childhood dreams had indeed come to nothing. Yet, in admitting that reality, especially to someone she hardly knew, she felt a burden being lifted.

What John said next, though, wasn't what she could've anticipated in a million years.

"Mine didn't either," he said, "and I'm glad."

"You're glad they didn't?"

He nodded. "I made a lot of mistakes in my life, but one wasn't being bound to dreams I had as a child. I mean, what did I know about life back then?"

Molly took a moment to absorb this then asked, "But if you let go of your dreams, what do you have left?"

"Oh, I still have them. I just created new dreams as an adult."

I just created new dreams as an adult. The logic was unassailable, but the solution seemed too simple. Too flimsy to hold back a lifetime of regrets; of midnight awakenings due to an irrepressible pressure in her chest; of half-depressed, half-envious feelings that accompanied her reading, seeing, hearing about someone who had made *her* wishes a reality. That someone who wasn't Molly Valle of Small Town, Mississippi. That someone *else*, the interloper, the thief of her dreams.

Logic couldn't defeat such ugly thoughts, and, to her great shame, Molly knew they were ugly. Neither could justifications—you never had the chance, you weren't in the right place at the right time, your responsibilities took too much of your time—defeat such feelings. Justifications that sounded weaker with each passing year. No, not even time itself could heal the pain of unfulfilled dreams; it could only half-bury it with accumulated years like a scar over traumatized tissue.

Now, John Pressman, with eight casually thrown out words—"I just created new dreams as an adult"—had obliterated that pain and disappointment. Was the man naive, callous, or did he indeed see something that most other people could not? To see more deeply and, in that depth of understanding, perceived the solution to

unfulfilled childhood desires? *I just created new dreams as an adult.*
Could it really be *that* simple?

"So, what was your old childhood dream?" Molly asked, probing.

"To advance in my old career."

"Which was?"

"Guess."

Molly studied him a long moment. Like everything else with
him, the answer must confound expectations. He was surely aware
of the impression his lumberjack's torso and Popeye's forearms
made. Furthermore, his chin scar added an unexpected subplot to
the friendly face. Was that acquired on the job?

No, Molly mentally chided his grinning face, *I will not say what
you think I'll say: "You're a construction worker."* What most people,
she'd imagine, would say.

Except that wasn't what Molly would've said. Although his
physique looked like it was built to be grasping a jackhammer,
she thought he was more suited to be contemplating a pond
festooned with water lilies, his unkempt blond hair squeezed
beneath a beret, one enormous hand delicately holding an easel
of paints. But what 19th-century French Impressionist, even from
lugging around his painting equipment all day, had a body like
John's?

"Give up?" His playful smile had widened. "I'll give you a hint.
During my old job, I used to lift a lot of heavy things made from cast
iron."

Cast iron? As in barbells and weight plates? John as a gym instruc-
tor or a high school coach? No, that seemed all wrong. *What creative*

art requires the lifting of heavy metal, though? A sculptor of cast-iron artwork doesn't lift it but ... sculpts it, right?

Then it came to her, improbable though the answer was. What was it that Sherlock Holmes once said? "Once you eliminate the impossible, whatever remains, no matter how improbable, must be the truth."

"You were a chef," Molly told John Pressman.

His reaction wasn't what she'd expected: widened eyes followed by incredulous guffaws. Instead, he simply said, "You're right. How did you know?"

"Your hint," she said, shocked that she'd gotten it right. "I figured you're involved in some sort of artistic endeavor, and the only artistic job I could think of that requires you to lift heavy cast-iron things is one involving pots and pans."

"Let the cat out of the bag too early, didn't I?"

"Maybe. But how many people have correctly guessed your old job before?"

"Not counting you, I'd say the number is ... zero point zero."

Molly laughed, and John joined her. It was the free, spontaneous laughter among friends. *The kind,* she thought, *where you don't try to control the odd snort or unseemly squeal.*

When that easy laughter subsided, she asked, "Were you any good?" She tried to imagine him decked out in a chef's whites, his unruly hair constricted inside the high white hat. "Sorry, that came out wrong. Of course, you were good. It's just that it's hard to imagine you as a chef, even if I guessed right."

"I can cook for you one of these days. Can't guarantee it's going to be to your liking, but I'm sure it'll be better than what we had an hour ago."

"I'd like that. To see how good your skills are." She thought that didn't sound right so she swiftly added, "In the kitchen."

John either didn't notice the faux pas or—bless his heart—ignored it. Instead, he said, "Just a bit above average, I'm afraid. But the beauty of it is not many people's palates, not even most reviewers', are developed enough to tell the merely good from the spectacular. By the time I quit, I was executive chef of a French restaurant on the top floor of Rockefeller Center."

"You were? I thought you said your dreams never came true."

"They didn't. When I finally achieved them, I felt none of the emotions I thought I would. No happiness, no excitement, none of the things I feel on a daily basis now. In fact, I would say—and I know this will sound contrary to what most people believe—that all the good things came to my life after I'd abandoned my childhood dreams and started living adult ones."

Molly swallowed this, like nutritious food that was disagreeable in taste. "And what are those adult dreams?" she asked him.

"Nothing but what my younger self would consider clichés. But the crux of the matter is some things are clichés because they're timeless truths. That the greatest excitement in life comes from helping out people every day, and that there's magic and adventure everywhere as long as you look deeply enough. These simple, down-to-earth lessons I forgot while working atop Rockefeller Center, but I guess I can be partly excused. It's hard to see deeply into anything from a quarter-mile up."

She nodded and knew what he meant but only in a nebulous kind of way. She thought again of those outlandish, dino-era visions she'd had earlier.

"What do you mean by 'looking deep enough'?" she asked.

"To answer that question," he said, "I first have to ask you one, 'When was the most exciting period of your life?'"

Molly blinked and felt like the proverbial deer caught in the headlights. Her reaction, though, wasn't because she didn't know the answer. She knew. Indeed, she had always known. It was just nobody had ever asked her such a question before or anything remotely in the same area code. And she had always *wanted* people to ask her such questions. Friends, family, past lovers, everyone.

But they never did, and on those rare occasions when she made such inquiries, all she ever received were blank stares or hasty segues into topics more concrete and less spiritual. *Safer* topics. For the people of her town—and she would guess the vast majority of humanity—observed the world not with their minds and imagination but solely with their eyes, which was a severe limitation.

A person's eyes, after all, could only see so far. To the nearest store to see what to buy. To the nearest restaurant to see what to eat. Destinations that provided life-saving musts—clothing, food, subsistence. But this was 1961, not the Stone Age, and men and women—especially women, Molly guessed—wanted more. Fulfillment not only of the body but of the mind and the soul, and the first step was having discussions that veered off the well-trodden path of who should win Friday night's football game.

"When was I most excited about life?" she said to John, the stranger who seemed more her friend than her oldest friend. "That's easy. When I was a young girl till my late twenties."

"Why?"

Why? The answer had always been easy, but she hadn't had time to dwell on it till now.

"Because when you're young, the world is always new," she said. "Everything seems to have a shiny surface to it, and you think life will always be like this. You will always be young, and you will always be experiencing new and exciting things. But once you get older, you find out life isn't like that. You will get old, and those shiny things will lose their luster. It's like once you've experienced enough of the world, you become … well, not sick of it exactly but more accustomed to it. Do you know what I mean?"

John nodded and listened to her. Really listened. Unlike most men who only listened till the time they could speak again.

"I think you've hit it right on the head," he told her. "But what if I tell you every single day for the rest of your life can be exciting in the same way as when you were a kid?"

Molly felt something move on her face, and she realized she must've involuntarily formed a disbelieving frown. She smoothed out her face and asked, "How's that?"

"By seeing what's shiny and beautiful isn't on the surface of things but *beneath* them."

She felt that incredulous frown trying to regain a foothold on her face. The conversation had gone off that well-trodden road all right. So off-road, it had crashed through bushes, crossed a piranha-infested river, and was now upside-down in a gully somewhere, its tires spinning helplessly. What exactly *was* he talking about?

"You mean the things we see every day?" she asked. "Even in the most mundane places?"

"Yup, even in the most mundane places. There are stories and magic behind everything."

Molly observed the sincerity in that rough-hewn, handsome face. Her skepticism remained or even intensified, but she felt something else. Something like an ice-covered climber steadily ascending her spine—a cool, low-grade thrill of sorts. John Pressman had put her on the spot by asking her to guess his former profession, and she decided it was time to return the favor.

"How about the diner we were just at, John? You think you can find magic there?"

"Especially there," he answered immediately.

Oh really? "Tell me."

"I don't need to tell you. You'll be able to see it yourself. Just close your eyes."

She hesitated a moment then did as she was told. And saw her second vision of the day.

CHAPTER 9

MOLLY

What Molly saw:

Nothing. Nothing at all. Or rather the fading sunlight, a uniform reddish-brown, filtered through closed eyelids. She waited ten seconds, thirty seconds, a full minute, feeling silly, wondering when she could open her eyes without offending John. She was still dwelling on this question when she realized she was no longer seeing the russet sunset but something darker, then darker still, then a depthless darkness.

Well, this is interesting. Like hypnosis minus the swinging watch. In this obsidian landscape, sound itself seemed to recede—the birds, the river, the wind—as did smell, until all was silent, scentless, and serene.

She wasn't sure how long she stayed in this state. A second, a minute, a millennium? Time seemed not so much elastic but wholly unimportant here. What was notable, though, were images and sounds that began to slowly push out the mute pitch-blackness. Then she realized she was back in the diner where she and John had eaten an hour earlier.

Except the diner wasn't the diner exactly, more like reality as interpreted through dreams. Some things were ... off. The lunch counter was not facing the entrance but was perpendicular to it. The clientele was not the usual interstate truckers but couples and families. And the place was certainly cleaner than it had been in real life.

Yet, in a manner difficult to describe, Molly felt the diner she observed in her mind was more real than the actual place, more in keeping with the original *idea* of that restaurant, unsullied by other people's or even her own earlier, mistaken interpretation.

Freed from unreliable senses like sight and sound and smell, she could indeed discern the essence of that diner, much like someone wise could see through another person's adorned exterior and affected poses to understand his or her true self. Against this overwhelming truth, what did it matter if a few stools and tables weren't in their "right" places?

Keeping her eyes closed but seeing more than she ever had, Molly realized that, while she could observe everything in the diner, she was not a part of it. Not as a customer, not as a passerby, not even as a person but rather a ... what? *A hummingbird*—the thought arriving in an instant, its initial absurdity rapidly giving way to complete certainty. Yes, a hummingbird with a gossamer body and wings flapping noiselessly.

Perfect and unseen, it flew languidly about the diner, directing its attention here and there, to one item before moving on to the next. The yellowed Formica counter, the too-white dentures of a laughing gray-haired man, the shiny tailfins of a parked Chevy Impala seen outside the window. Then it circled back to what it had examined a couple of times before—or rather, to *whom*.

The blond, surly, middle-aged waitress. The woman who had served John and Molly an hour earlier—she was in this vision, if this could indeed be called a vision. Molly wasn't sure what she was seeing via the hummingbird's eyes, but she did know this: she could observe this woman in far more detail now than she had in reality. The way she walked, straight-legged and purposeful, like a drill sergeant. How much more deeply etched the wrinkles around her pinched mouth were than in her laughter-induced crow's feet. How she was so impatient in taking orders and delivering food but didn't seem at all anxious to get home.

Molly had missed all these details earlier, including an eight-inch-long burn mark that ran along the woman's left forearm. The scar didn't look recent, but then Molly was no nurse. What had caused the woman's burn? And when? Answering these two questions seemed all-important, not only in deciphering the woman's personality but in unearthing the purpose of this vision. And so Molly concentrated on the few cubic inches of the burn, and everything beyond them began to blur into a half-painted backdrop.

As she fixated on the woman's scar, though, she suddenly realized the unburned flesh of the forearm had become less lined and more youthful. Molly pulled back then and saw it was still the waitress, except a two-decade younger version, her mouth no longer pinched, her sweaty face with nary a wrinkle. She, in fact, could no longer be called a waitress.

Outfitted in a grease-streaked denim uniform and working the handwheel on a piece of heavy machinery—it was a turret lathe, Molly thought, though she had no idea how she knew this—the woman was a real-life Rosie the Riveter, except her actual name was Kelly as shown by her nametag. Kelly, who at around twenty-five was tired, dirty, and … happy. Yes, happy, a state so different from her middle-aged sulk. And behind her, not in a diner but in an immense factory of machines and half-constructed boats, was an army of similarly exhausted and happy women.

Kelly burned her arm here. Like the knowledge of the turret lathe, Molly had no idea from where this information originated. She just *knew*, and she accepted this truth.

Just like she knew this clanking, hammering, shouting landscape was the Higgins Industries ship factory in New Orleans, and that the overturned hulls her hummingbird flew over would become the landing craft that transported the V and VII Corps on D-Day fifteen months later. Just knew that the women, overworked and muscle-strained, would often, years later, see this moment in *their* factory as a high point in their lives, when the necessities of war production swept away the lies of female weakness and mechanical ineptitude. Just knew that Kelly had burned her arm here, but the *how* wasn't important for she saw the injury as an indelible reminder of when both her mind and body were free from society's restraints.

But those boundaries began to reappear just as Molly's hummingbird returned to Kelly. The woman was no longer in smeared workman's denims but in a green housedress, her face still young and now clean, but that eventual, middle-aged melancholy had already planted its first flag on that visage. On the table beside her was a newspaper, its huge, joyful headline half-obscured by a pink slip of paper. Molly didn't need to read the slip to know what it said, but she willed the hummingbird forward all the same.

Except the bird itself had become immobilized and could only view the proceedings from the apparent vantage point of a cuckoo in an old clock above the fireplace. But there was no fireplace in this new location—no longer the factory but a small, cramped apartment with almost deliberately mismatched furniture. Morning Louisiana sunlight poured in through the patchy blinds and made whitish pools on the dark floor. The air was still, and all was quiet. Too quiet and too still, as if the apartment had gone into hibernation, and Kelly was waiting, angrily and hopelessly, for it to awaken.

Into this world of despondent stillness came an almost mocking display of animation. A young man emerged from the hallway. There was nothing distinguishing about his face except a too-wide, oblivious smile, which appeared like a white plate laid atop the tall, blue pedestal that was his denim clothes. He was carrying a lunch pail, and as he put a yellow cap over his black crewcut, Molly realized this man, Kelly's husband returned from the war, had stolen his wife's uniform.

No, that wasn't quite right. It wasn't the exact uniform, after all, and *he* hadn't stolen it. No, society had, and what it had stolen was a lot more than cotton fabric and clothes dye. Not that this man, good-natured but unobservant like most men of his generation, of all generations maybe, could see this fact. Still, when he glanced toward his wife, his smile faltered a bit.

War's over, honey, he told her. Factory don't need you gals no more.

In the vision, Molly sensed more than heard these words. She also knew he was called Lionel and that the name had caused him to be teased as a kid.

It's not like you lost your job 'cause I got it now, Lionel explained. No response from Kelly. If I was you, I'd be in hog heaven right about now, he ventured on. Don't need to wake up at the crack of dawn to go to some stinky, dangerous factory. Ain't got to worry about burns no more neither. No response. Wish I could stay home all day, do whatever I wanted. Go shopping, get my hair and nails done. Then, finally, there *was* a response.

At her husband's list of imagined female interests, Kelly turned to him and just stared. Not a stare of hostility but incredulity—a kaleidoscope of incredulity whose biggest colored bead was a single thought: *How could this man, whom I married, know me so, so little?*

Lionel must've seen that incomprehension and felt the resultant discomfort for he looked away and muttered, Suit yourself. The banging screen door heralded his departure.

Kelly remained sitting and watching the closed screen door. In the again still and quiet apartment, Molly watched her watch. As inanimate as the objects in the room, Kelly had become a statue, a Venus de Milo but with arms and a crushing despondency. Her eyes blinked, moistened, and when they blinked again, a single tear slid down her right cheek.

Or, more accurately, *began* to slide down for the tear moved far more slowly than it would have in reality. With each quarter-inch of movement, a year seemed to pass, that stretch of time transforming Kelly's face little by little. The downward trail of the tear became like a real trail through a landscape, though one made of skin and the curvature of cheekbone. And like the terrain around a real trail, the passage of time changed everything. Not in the growth of trees or buildings but in the depth and increase of wrinkles, the softening of skin, and the sagging of the jawline. By the time the tear had run itself out, down the length of her face and halfway down her neck, Kelly was no longer the happy factory worker of twenty-five or the despondent housewife of thirty but what she had become: the despondent, pinch-mouthed waitress of middle age.

Molly watched her stand up, no longer in the green dress but in her waitress getup with its white apron and the tied-back hair, the constricted strands half white themselves. The apartment looked the same, static and quiet, but in some fundamental way, it wasn't. A sense that this was all there was and always would be had pervaded the place, and when Kelly left to go to work, she was the one who banged the screen door shut.

CHAPTER 10

MOLLY

The world was black then brown then orange.

Molly opened her eyes and blinked, the orange being the final, yielding rays of the sun smothered at last by the night. She was lying on her back, and as she sat up, she found herself again on a bluff overlooking the Mississippi River. The real world.

Except the "real world" her eyes observed wasn't any more *real* than the vision she'd witnessed with her mind. In fact, it seemed less real, less substantial, faded even. Much like one's waking hours paled in comparison to the domain of dreams, and actual landscapes never had the intensity of colors as their Kodachrome reproductions.

If something is more real than reality, why then should reality still be crowned real and that something else denigrated as unreal?

She didn't know the answer to that question and even, after

thinking it, questioned its validity. For there was something more real than reality that her eyes, not her mind, were currently observing. An entity that had shape, that was solid, yet possessed the same punch as the extraordinary images of her visions. And it—*he*—was sitting cross-legged and smiling at her.

"Oh, my God," Molly said to John. "You wouldn't believe what I saw."

He nodded, encouraging her, the setting sun a campfire glow in each eye.

"Well, what I saw was," she began eagerly, and just as eagerly stopped herself. *How does one proceed without sounding like a ... what? A lunatic. Yes, a straitjacketed, confined-to-a-rubber-room, thinking-one-was-Napoleon's-pet-poodle lunatic.*

"I found out how she got that burn mark," she finally offered. Lamely, she thought a split-second later.

John nodded as if he understood what she was babbling about. Then he said something that made her realize he *did* understand: "Now that you mentioned it, I think our waitress did have a burn on her left arm."

"That's right, but I don't remember seeing it back at the diner. But I did see it in my ... dream. I'm just not sure whether what I saw was the truth or just my imagination."

"Does it matter?"

She was about to say, "Of course, it does," but stopped herself.

Then he voiced the exact thoughts she was chewing over: "What difference does it make whether it was true or not? The surface specifics don't matter, but—"

"—the underlying truth does," Molly finished for him, recalling what he had earlier told her.

He nodded again. "Stories that are waiting to be discovered and explored and enjoyed. They're all around us, if we just look deeply enough."

"The story I saw wasn't a happy one."

"If every story were happy, life would be awfully uninteresting."

"Maybe," Molly said, not quite conceding the point. Every story being happy sounded quite wonderful.

She adjusted herself on the blanket, drew her bare legs beneath her, got more comfortable. The short distance separating her body from his, a couple of feet maybe, seemingly contained not air but something tangible and warm. That she was attracted to him was an overwhelming certainty and, she hoped, vice versa. But here, for the first time, was something new. Something that had supplanted the physical pull—a magnetism of the mind.

She liked the act of talking to John Pressman, though it wasn't talking for talking's sake, which characterized every other conversation she'd ever had with men. No, this was talking as grand exploration, Livingstone seeking the source of the Nile, Ponce De León the Fountain of Youth. Except the unmapped territories here were their own minds, whose boundless topography rivaled any country's.

She could see herself decked out in an explorer's khakis, shouldering a Victorian-era knapsack and carrying a compass. Could see herself wading through hippo-infested rivers, sitting atop camels traversing moonlit sand dunes, standing in wonderment before a Neolithic pillar with its millennia-old reliefs of animals ...

All these splendid images and more, like grains of sand in all the deserts of the world, contained inside a single mind, just waiting to be discovered.

"Isn't it a bit exhausting, though?" Molly found herself saying, still dazzled by all she wanted to know about John.

"What is?"

"Always trying to see below the surface of things?"

"At the beginning maybe, but with time, it becomes second nature. It was always a cakewalk when we were kids. We just need to rediscover this gift."

"And have you rediscovered it?"

"Heck no," John said and laughed. His laugh was genuine, as was his modesty—Molly sensed there would never be a time when he was insincere or false in any way—but she wasn't sure if his self-assessment was correct.

Then he said something that threw her for a loop: "I feel like sometimes my life is just beginning. Don't you?"

At this question, Molly smiled, but she knew her smile was off-kilter. John was a lot of things, but with his graying temples and lined face, young wasn't one of them. And neither was she.

"In two years, I'm going to be fifty," she told him, surprised she'd divulged her age so freely.

"So?"

So ... so? So indeed. But it wasn't that simple.

She considered the question a second and realized where the problem lay. While a man could conceivably feel he was in his prime in his forties or even fifties—though certainly not the "beginning" of his life—a woman would think the idea insane. It was a wretched double standard, and it was displayed everywhere.

She thought of the last movie she'd seen, *North by Northwest*, where a gray-haired Cary Grant wooed a very blond and very young Eva Marie Saint. And Cary Grant was still considered a sophisticated leading man, whereas a woman in her fifties with gray hair would be unthinkable as an appealing love interest.

Yes, it was unfair, monstrously unfair, but how could she express these views without sounding like the bitter old maid that she suspected a lot of men thought she was, those bastards.

"I can't be young again," Molly found herself saying, and hoped she'd squelched the resignation implicit in that statement.

"I don't mean we're ever going to be young again," John said. "And I don't mean what society thinks and says either because it's often wrong. What I believe is, to put a spin on the old saying, what's good for the gander is doubly good for the goose."

Molly wanted to kiss him then, an almost overwhelming need. It was as if he had a telegraph machine in his head—one that sent personalized messages to alleviate all her pains and fears as they came to her. But the opposite reaction to her sudden smile came too and, alongside that need, a reflexive wetness in her eyes. She looked away and was glad she felt John doing the same, both ostensibly to look at the sunset, where the final rays streaked across the sky like fuchsia chalk marks on a blackboard.

"No, we can't be young again, and I don't want to be," she heard John say. "I've spent an entire lifetime finding myself, and I don't want to be lost again. Youth is indeed wasted on the young."

Molly turned back to him and nodded. She had long known George Bernard Shaw's famous saying but only began to understand it after her mid-thirties, when the reality of life finally hit her. Not the "reality" of youth and beauty and optimism, and all the glorious things that came with the naiveté of the unseasoned. No, she had been there, and while youth's ignorance was indeed bliss, she didn't want to return to that half-knowledge.

She now knew what she hadn't known or even thought likely as a young woman. That after the age of thirty, certainly after forty, life became a series of small triumphs and major heartbreaks. The death of parents, possible divorce, the slow but inevitable collapse of the body, and the disillusionment then the death of dreams. Youth was nothing but an idyllic island before the coming typhoon of middle and late age.

Yet, despite all these depressing truths, Molly didn't want to become young again. John was right about that. She didn't want to live in ignorance. She wanted to be cognizant of what life really was and to enjoy it without illusions.

And she suspected, indeed hoped, that the man in front of her would be able to bestow this priceless gift to her.

"I've spent fifty years of my life searching for answers," John told her, "often wasting years, even decades, going down blind alleys. Like I've said earlier, I don't know everything, but I do think I have a decent handle on what life is now. I can enjoy a summer sunset, a nice meal, the company of interesting, intelligent people. Can enjoy all these things without the confusion of youth. That's why I feel my life is just beginning."

Molly nodded, dwelling on his words. And as she became cognizant of that face and the thick neck and rounded shoulders that propped it up, she realized she was no longer *only* attracted to his mind. The physical had returned again, and she was aware how close, how achingly close, she was to John, with his absurdly masculine body and cutlass-sharp mind.

She felt a sudden desire—and the image almost caused her to laugh out loud—to crawl lioness-like to him, steady her hands on his broad shoulders, and plant her lips on his. Those sensitive lips surrounded and accentuated by the slight stubble, gold and gray hairs interspersed, and the zigzag of that white, slightly raised flesh of his chin scar. Those lips that must taste as delectable as the salted rim of a margarita glass on a sweltering summer day.

But she also knew if she kissed him and he kissed back, they wouldn't be able to stop, and though a part of her would relish it like a desert traveler welcoming a first gulp of oasis water, another part of her—the part long calcified by reality—added a counterweight to her desire.

For the kiss would indeed lead to something else, and *that* would surely last beyond the time the sky would turn a star-studded black. She was sure some people could find their way back by starlight alone, but she wouldn't bet that she and John could. And while a night under the stars sounded delicious, a part of her remained forty-eight years old, with a forty-eight-year-old's next-day responsibilities, including being there for a ten o'clock tutoring session with a certain overgrown teenager.

Besides, an unfamiliar, impish voice told her, *good things come to those who wait.*

Molly found herself saying, "You know what would be perfect now?"

"A flashlight?" John replied immediately.

She laughed then, both relieved and disappointed by his answer. He had read her mind again and given her—given *them*—an easy way out.

Under the purpling sky, they picked up their empty beer bottles and wrapped up the blanket and then headed back to the diner's parking lot. She found it hard to see the path in the dimming light, but somehow, her four other senses had become magnified. The world was awash with the sounds, smells, and touch of the forest. She felt she could even taste the surrounding trees and brush, like sweet sap.

Except sap wasn't sweet, was it? Molly was sure it wasn't, but then it didn't matter. Like the vision earlier, her imagination might've been getting to her, but the underlying truth wasn't any less valid. She had never felt more alive in her entire life than at this moment. Not at eighteen, not at twenty-one, not at twenty-seven, never. No, it was now, at forty-eight years, five months, and twenty-six days of age, striding under a fragranced canopy of tree boughs not five miles from her house, with a man whom she suspected she might actually love walking behind her.

Halfway to the diner's parking lot, she realized something else. She'd been inhabiting a new role for the past several hours. A role she had once played, like the lead in a great play, but had long neglected. A familiar role that, because of its prolonged absence, now felt startlingly new and wonderful. Not a teacher, not a daughter, and God knows, not Miss Upright Citizen of Small Town, Mississippi.

No, Molly felt one thing and one thing only:

A woman.

She felt like a woman again.

CHAPTER 11

MOLLY

Molly was driving home alone in the dark. Earlier, John had driven back to the college, and they had said their goodbyes, with great reluctance and no small sense of relief. She didn't know what could've happened if they had stayed together longer, and she didn't feel she was ready to find out quite yet either.

The windows were down, and the night outside—a living Van Gogh's *Starry Night* of towering tree silhouettes under a canvas of stars—pushed in its balmy fragrance and stereophonic cicada choruses.

She drove with her left hand, her right resting on her bare right leg. A leg that, with its nearly half-century accumulation of wrinkles and cellulite, she hadn't thought of as being pretty or even feminine for a long, long time. Instead, its flesh and bones were only a means to an end—locomotion. As had the word "woman" been to her for so long. A biological term, a female human being, no more alluring or mysterious than the diagram in a high school physiology book. Faded ink lines on musty paper.

But while that description was accurate in describing how Molly had felt for decades, it wasn't enough. No, it wasn't nearly enough. It was too denuded of a woman's essence and power. For "woman" wasn't only defined by staid scientists but also by poets, painters, and musicians throughout millennia.

By artists who wrote Homeric epics and Shakespearean sonnets, painted *Girl with a Pearl Earring*, composed *The Marriage of Figaro*, directed *Casablanca*. A "woman" who could set off a war between Bronze Age city-states in the Mediterranean, a "woman" capable of seducing not one but two Roman dictators to secure her own power, a "woman" who could inspire a Corsican corporal to conquer most of 18th-century Europe …

All these experiences, whether historical or fiction, made the life of a woman magical. A woman could walk out her front door and begin the game, the most blessedly exciting game in existence. The game she had, since the onset of adulthood, played with the clumsy, rough, yet irresistible opposite sex. The game that went back hundreds of centuries to the dawn of history. The fashions and etiquettes might've changed—from loincloth to togas to Elizabethan corsets to the JCPenney mail-order dress she was wearing—but the underlying truth remained the same. It was hyperbole, sure, but what was hyperbole but an amplification of truth?

This was a truth she had first become aware of during her sophomore year in high school, when her blouses had tightened around her chest. She began noticing boys and was, in turn, noticed *by* boys. She discovered that she was no longer invisible—a large-diameter spotlight had formed above her. And though she had always been a private person and in general didn't crave attention, she still enjoyed the *possibility* of men's attention. The spotlight, constant and never-ending, shone with enviable intensity on her. Men fawned over her, took her out to dinner, and the light even led a handsome law school student to ask her to marry him.

During those years of marriage, whose unhappiness ultimately became oppressive, she hadn't noticed the spotlight had dimmed. Hadn't noticed until her mid-thirties when she divorced, and the men were no longer there. She, like most young women, had assumed the spotlight would always be there. She hadn't known that in life, a woman only had a decade, maybe two if she was lucky, of being a woman of the poets and artists and not a woman of the biology textbook.

So, so unfair, she had thought, how short that magical moment was, not even a quarter of the average woman's lifespan. Her twenty-ish—or, worse, her teenage—self had been so naïve. To have assumed the spotlight would always be there, forever, like in a fairy tale. At thirty-five, she thought she had finally figured out what it meant to be a woman, and it was a return to the invisibility of prepubescent girlhood while remaining in a grown body and with a grown body's responsibilities. Such was a woman's life and fate.

Now, at forty-eight years of age, Molly realized her thirty-five-year-old self had been wrong. Staggeringly wrong. No, the spotlight had always been there—was indeed shining on her as she drove—

and it would always be there. Her teenage and twentyish selves had been right, but they hadn't understood *how* they'd been right.

The spotlight hadn't dimmed as Molly aged but had changed its glow instead. It had grown more intense with each new experience, had become more personalized and distinguished. It was no longer the bland whitish light of youth, a light dictated by a ceaselessly shallow society and therefore able to be seen by everyone in such a society. No, hers at present was a spotlight with highly individualized rays that could no longer be seen by most men simply because most men's eyes weren't *good* enough to see them.

As she drove, she surprised herself with a sudden laugh. How blind, infinitely blind, she had been to think that men's inability to see her forty-eight-year-old self was a regret or, worse, a failing on her own part. No, what it really was was a blessing, for that inability had separated the wheat from the chaff. The spotlight was indeed always there but only for someone perceptive enough, brave enough, mature enough to see it still shining above her head.

Someone, Molly suspected, she had met a day earlier in a diner not a ten-minute drive from the empty house to which she was now heading, on roads she had ridden on thousands of times before.

CHAPTER 12

MOLLY

A half-century later, when Molly recalled the five days separating her first date with John Pressman from her second, she thought of the eye inside a tropical cyclone—a brief period of respite. Except it wasn't a harmful storm but a life-affirming one. Its hurricane-force winds left behind not destruction but rather a layer of Technicolor over all the aspects of her life. And within this world of oversaturated colors and senses and emotions, she began living again.

Reading *Hawaii*, the latest bestseller from James Michener, and seeing and hearing its glorious Polynesian characters as if they were standing in her living room. Pulling weeds in her small backyard and planting gardenias and black-eyed Susans. Watching *The Jack Benny Show* on TV and laughing as hard as she had thirty years earlier when it was only a radio show. Taking cold baths to cool her body while drinking cold beer to cool her mind. Fixing up her

Schwinn bicycle, long entombed in her garage like some Babylonian artifact, and taking it out on after-dinner rides.

How had she missed the beauty of these everyday, once ho-hum actions? She didn't know, but she did know how she'd rediscovered their splendor. It was John. Of course, it was John. Along with this realization came that ever-present thought: *It's now Tuesday. In four days, I'll see him.* Then: *It's now Wednesday. In three days ...*

Not that Molly *didn't* see him. He was in the local papers almost daily, among more sit-ins, arrests, and meetings. She wanted to see him, but she knew her presence would be too distracting and counterproductive at such a crucial moment. There was much more coverage now, the kind that small Southern towns didn't like, and there were even rumors of a march among the Negro population. And since blacks made up half of the town's population, she didn't see how the world she had always known could remain so for long.

Half the population, she thought and felt an immeasurable shame. They were invisible, just as described in that recent bestseller by Ralph Ellison. They were invisible because we were conditioned—no, we *forced* ourselves—to not see them. "We" and "they"—the insulting yet undeniably real demarcation between the two populations. Or *was* it real? Or was it like so many other things that society deemed concrete but were as insubstantial as a glass of water spilled into Lake Pontchartrain? She thought she knew the answer, and she wanted to test it out.

She parked her Plymouth in the half-empty parking lot with the ill-defined boundaries. Through the windshield, she saw the trio of buildings—a barbershop, a Chinese restaurant, a food market—that made up this minuscule shopping center. She had always known of this place but had never gone, it being hidden behind an ancient Burma Shave billboard far from the highway. Plus, it was squarely on the wrong side of the tracks, which meant nothing to her now. Considering how the place's proprietors, whoever they were, seemed indifferent to the color of people's hands as long as they held green, being there indeed felt very, very right—and exciting.

Here again is John's maxim: look deeply enough and you'd see the beauty beneath the surface of things. Even at a small, rundown food market on the edge of town.

She was inside a quarter-hour, humming to herself and pushing her cart down aisles indistinguishable from whites-only markets but also vastly different due to the place's multiracial clientele—a few Negroes and whites shopping alongside each other and not caring at all—when she heard her name: "Miss Vail."

She turned and was startled. "Cash, what are you doing here?"

Her former student was standing there, so constricted inside a striped polo shirt, he looked like an insect about to molt. A very nervous insect. He continuously glanced about, seemingly expecting a predator to pounce. Molly couldn't blame him. He was, after all, the son of the chief of police, and *that* person wasn't very welcome in *this* part of town.

"I followed you, Miss Vail," the sixteen-year-old boy said and gulped. "I didn't mean to, but I just had to see you and tell you why I can't be your student anymore."

"I know. Your mom called me."

"Yeah," he said, his eyes fixed on the floor. "I'm sorry about that."

"Don't apologize," she said, and she too looked about. She was glad the market, on a weekday morning, was reasonably empty.

"I told Mama that you were the best teacher I ever had." Then, as if forcing the words out before he could change his mind, he said, "She doesn't know why you're doing what you're doing."

"I'm not doing anything."

"But you are. You *are*. Mama said a friend of hers saw you at a diner the other night. With a Yankee agitator."

"I—" Molly stopped herself. She wasn't about to explain her dating habits to a boy.

In any case, he didn't seem to notice that she had stopped talking. He seemed off in his own realm, talking to himself, trying to convince himself of something.

"Everything was so perfect the way it was, Miss Vail, before them Yankees came down and mucked everything up. It was so perfect—"

"Perfect for whom, Cash? Perfect for whom?"

"Why, for us—" Then it was the boy who ceased talking.

She could see him thinking, could almost see the gears of his mathematically inclined brain grappling with social currents and injustice.

Finally, he shook his head, as if clearing away some distasteful images. "I just don't understand it. All I know is the town's falling apart, and Mama and Daddy seem to be at the end of their tether." The boy appeared on the verge of tears. "Everything's just so damn confusing."

Molly wanted to hug him but steeled herself not to. Instead, she said, "Things have always been confusing. It's just that we've lied to ourselves that they haven't been." She almost added, *Beneath the surface of things*, but caught herself. He wouldn't understand.

"How do you know what this town's really like?" Cash asked, his eyes suddenly on hers. For the first time in her life, she sensed a latent anger in the boy, like a reddened blister about to pop. "How do you know this when everybody else I know tells me different?"

"Sometimes, you just know. You have to look deep inside yourself and see the truth there, and it doesn't matter if everybody else says otherwise. Just like I know you're not meant for football but for math and science. You're meant to be the engineer you once told me you wanted to be."

A grown man's furrows divided the boy's forehead. His eyes were shimmering, his anger dissipated but not his confusion. Those wet eyes looked away for a second then returned to her again.

"You really believe that, Miss Vail?"

"With all my heart, Cash."

"Then you're as big a fool as my parents say you are!"

Without another word, he swung around and strode away, his Bluto-from-Popeye physique nearly blocking the whitish doorway as he exited the market into the sun-blinding world outside. Molly watched him go and knew the boy she'd always known was gone forever.

"You sure know how to win them over," someone said from behind her.

She turned and blinked, for a few heartbeats not believing what she was seeing. That it could be *her* seemed fantastic, but the mirage didn't disappear. John's sassy sidekick was pushing her own shopping cart toward her. The coincidence seemed too great, and it was, Molly later reflected, for fiction. But such coincidences happened all the time in reality. And this had to be reality, for Molly could never have imagined the woman's getup: a black-and-white, polka-dotted pantsuit bisected by a yellow tie with a matching yellow cloche hat.

"Bethanee," Molly said.

"So, you remember my name?" The young woman nodded toward the half-full cart. "We didn't get our skulls cracked last night, and to celebrate, John's gonna cook dinner for us. I'm the designated shopper."

"How are things going for you?"

"Oh, I'm sure you've read about it in the papers, right? Besides"—a crescent of white teeth—"you're gonna have your own dinner with John later this week, ain't you? I'm sure he'll feed you all the juicy bits you can swallow."

Molly caught her own frown. She had suspected Bethanee didn't like her, for whatever reason, but here was the confirmation.

Bethanee nodded toward the doorway. "That was the son of the cracker cop, wasn't it?"

Molly said nothing.

"He looked ready to fly off the handle. What happened? You gave him an F on an essay or something?" Bethanee laughed at her own joke, but her eyes weren't amused. "That boy. He a shitkicking bruiser like his daddy is?"

"No, he's not. You don't know anything about him. His father isn't a bruiser either."

"Could've fooled me, the way he arrested us, oh, three times now. Maybe you skipped that part in the papers."

Molly felt the woman's hostility like a physical force. Part of it, she had no doubt, was that Bethanee had a crush on John. Over twice her age, he nevertheless had bewitched her, though Molly knew he hadn't done so intentionally. His presence alone was enough, as Molly knew personally. Yet the young woman's aggression also emanated from some place else, directed at *what* Molly was as opposed to *who* she was.

"Of course," Bethanee continued, "if you wanna see how much *not* a bruiser your fuzz friend is, you can come along with us the next time we sit in."

"I just might do that."

To Molly's surprise, the young woman blinked and was, for a moment, quiet. *Called your bluff, didn't I,* Molly thought with no small amount of satisfaction.

"Oh, no, on second thought, I'd rather not have you along," Bethanee said, and her lips had reconfigured into that humorless smile again. "I don't wanna be shot."

"Shot?" Molly said and noticed a middle-aged Negro shopper pushing her cart a bit too briskly past, casting wary eyes on them both.

"Why, sure," Bethanee said breezily. "See, right now, I'm just an uppity colored girl getting above her station, which to the folks of this town should always be the outhouse. But you, a nice Southern belle? Why, you're one of them. You, they *detest*. So I'd rather be dropped into a barrel of live scorpions than be around you when we're downtown and surrounded by your townsfolk."

"What would you have me do then?"

"Why, I ain't got the foggiest. What your kind has always done, I guess. Look the other way. But then we came along, and suddenly you had a purpose in life. Now, ain't that special?"

"Everybody has to find a way to feel better about themselves, right?"

"That's—" Bethanee stopped talking. Her smile faltered then reasserted itself. But, like a puzzle only half-finished, it still missed important pieces.

Touché, Molly could see the young woman acknowledging.

"I guess I should be heading back now," Bethanee finally said. "I'll tell John I saw you and that you're *really* looking forward to this weekend."

Molly said goodbye and watched Bethanee wheel the cart away, the young woman's gait, whether affected or natural, belonging to a model on a runway.

You're really looking forward to this weekend.

Now, that was no lie. Molly smiled herself, shook her head, and continued her grocery-shopping.

CHAPTER 13

MOLLY

Three days later, Molly found herself at the market again, give or take a couple of feet from where she'd stood when she watched Bethanee leave. She was in the same location, but that was like saying the Mississippi of 1961 was the same as the Mississippi when Spanish conquistadors roamed. Hyperbole, true, she had to admit, but only by a small amount. John Pressman, after all, was pushing a shopping cart, like a dutiful housewife, right beside her.

"Would you like some pasta?" he asked, smiling, as he bent to some bottom shelves.

"I'll leave that decision to you," she said and felt she was in a dream.

But she knew she was in reality. John's tiredness was too real. There were bags under his eyes and even the rugged shoulders sagged a little. But his was a tiredness interwoven with happiness, and while she wished the entirety of his happiness had come from seeing her again, she knew otherwise. She had read the papers and knew how her town—well, the mayor, the city council, and, she hoped, Hollis—was finally open to discussions. John, Bethanee, and the other demonstrators appeared on the cusp of victory, which had allowed him to call Molly up and cook that dinner he'd promised.

So she followed him around the market, stopping periodically and watching as he reached out his strongman's hands and, with the daintiness of an Emily Post etiquette coach, picked up this or that food item. She had to stifle a chuckle each time. She had never known a man who so enjoyed activities that were seen as being traditionally feminine.

I'm in love, aren't I?

She thought she knew the answer by how much she wanted to be there. Wouldn't have traded being there for any other location in the world. Wouldn't have traded it for all the exotic destinations flaunted in Pan Am travel brochures. Not Tahiti, not Monte Carlo, not Hong Kong.

No, she wanted to be here, in this ramshackle market not a ten-minute drive from her humdrum house and life. Except it wasn't a humdrum life anymore, was it? *No, I'm at the most exciting place on Earth.* The center of the world. The Roman Forum during the reign of Augustus Caesar.

"Let's explore more," John said after he deposited a head of broccoli into the cart.

Explore more—as if the market were that millennia-past location that she'd just imagined and not just … well, a market in her hometown. How strange the sentiment yet how fitting too.

His aura is enveloping you, she thought and, with that aura, his powers of perception. For travel, she realized, was not merely a change of location but, more importantly, also a change of mind. All the pleasures and all the exoticism of travel could be accessed wherever one was. One just needed to step back and—she thought again of John's oft-repeated call—to look more deeply and see the newness behind the most unnoteworthy of places, including the market. This was magic in shopping aisle 3A.

Running parallel with these pleasant thoughts, though, was a nagging, unhappy one. She didn't want to bring it up, especially now, but she felt she had to, no matter how jarring the timing.

"I saw Bethanee here a week ago."

John nodded. "Yes, I know. She told me." He stopped pushing his cart and turned toward her. "She's a black woman who grew up in the South."

So he knew. Of course, he did. His short, explanatory sentence was enough.

She tried to imagine how Bethanee, well-read and nimble-minded, would feel growing up in such a society. Forget about Pan Am vacations abroad. How about simply buying bread from a downtown bakery? To know a vast part of the world was closed off to you yet remained open to others with far less brainpower and ability solely because their skin had less pigmentation. And any challenge to this immoral system would often be met by violence not only from fellow civilians but from the full powers of the state.

Langston Hughes's famous poem didn't go far enough. This

wasn't a dream deferred but one bludgeoned in the head and left bleeding in the gutter.

"We're not all like that," Molly said quietly to John. "White Southerners, I mean."

"I know. And I think Bethanee knows too."

An image—the young woman lingering a bit too long in the dorm foyer—came to Molly. "She likes you, you know."

"Does she?"

"You know she does."

"Yeah, I guess she does."

"Do you like her?" Molly asked and felt her teeth biting her lower lip.

He shook his head. "I do like her but not in that manner. She's about the same age my daughter would've been if I had followed the path of my high school friends. I don't think enough about not having kids to regret it. But occasionally I do. It would've been nice."

He began pushing the cart again, and Molly followed, glad the act of walking took her away from her own ruminations. But it wasn't enough. She couldn't help but tell herself that it would've been nice indeed to have had a child. Now, it was too late. *So there's one more connection between this man and me. We're both childless, and we'll both remain so.* With this melancholy thought, Molly felt a near-crushing tenderness for the man.

This good, sensitive man will be in my house soon. I'll be alone with him then. At last.

"I think we're finished here," John said, turning from his quarter-filled cart. "Do you need anything?"

She'd been staring down, past the streaked linoleum floor, to her own deep-buried contemplation. She looked up and said, "No, we can go if you want."

"Then let's get cooking." He smiled and headed toward the cashier. As Molly followed, on legs that felt like linguine cooked al-dente, she wondered what he meant by that.

CHAPTER 14

JOHN

He felt her beside him, not as a woman a foot or two down the kitchen counter but an inch away, a millimeter. Her presence was so much more powerful than her bodily self, fetching though that undoubtedly was. Her presence was part scent and part image, as glimpsed from the corner of his right eye. It was nearly overwhelming, making it hard to concentrate on what he needed to do. Worse, *all* parts of him were aware of her, including John Pressman Junior, who, uniform ironed and shoes polished, was standing ramrod-straight for inspection. *At ease, soldier*, he commanded it, but the private—his privates—continued its act of insubordination.

"So, what are you making?" Molly Valle asked, leaning forward on her countertop for a better look. "I'm expecting something magnificent, you know?"

"It's a secret," he told her, chopping vegetables, "but I assure you nothing less than magnificent is what you'll get."

He angled his body somewhat away from her so John Junior could be mostly hidden, and if it weren't for the embarrassment, he would've laughed. After millennia of evolution, the man with the loincloth and the bad teeth was still right below the surface.

But how could anyone blame him? God, she was beautiful! More so than he had remembered, if that was possible. He hadn't seen her in almost a week, and during that time, amid more sit-ins and inter-actions with the town's infuriated, hidebound citizens, when the ugliness of the world had been raw and immediate, he had thought of her.

He had envisioned each contour and line of her face, the spell-binding individuality of personal detail. Here was a woman who had lived, and that life had been kind and good. And within that good-ness lay true glamour, which was far more than the sum of ephem-eral, physical parts. That was why, even attired in an unpretentious house dress, her forty-eight-year-old face scarcely made up, Molly was glamorous in a way that put in the shade women half her age and on the cover of fashion magazines.

"A secret, huh?" this glamorous woman asked him. "Picked up from your chef days, right? Which brings me to a question I've been meaning to ask: why a chef?"

"I guess I just kind of fell into it. When you're born a poor Jewish boy on the wrong side of the tracks—the lower half of New York's East Side anyway—you grab whatever career comes along."

"You're Jewish?"

"Yup, and when I tell folks this, their next response is usually, 'But you don't look Jewish.'"

Molly smiled. "Oh, I wasn't going to say that. I'd imagine, like Southerners, Jews come in all shapes and sizes. I was just curious about the 'Pressman.'"

"I'm sure my parents rearranged the letters in their surname a bit at Ellis Island. Tried to blend in better, you know?"

"Did it work?"

"Let's just say a lot of the Italian and Polish kids I grew up with kept on calling me Mike, except they somehow forgot the name began with an M and not a K."

"God, how horrible," she said, seemed to consider something, then tentatively tapped her own chin. "Is that where ... ?"

He nodded and rubbed his chin scar. "I wish I could say what others would at this point: you should see the other kid. But the truth was, I lost more than I won. You see, I didn't have this amazing musculature back then."

Molly laughed then, a soft but genuine laugh that she clamped down on. "I'm sorry. I didn't mean to laugh."

"It's okay," he said and chuckled along with her. He glanced at her and wished he could run his tongue along her laugh lines then draw ever-tighter circles until it reached the centermost of her lips, where her own tongue would peek out and touch his like a rediscovered friend. Then he shoved that thought from his mind lest John Junior get perky again.

"So how did you get from the Lower East Side to the top of Rockefeller Center?"

"You remembered," he said, thinking, *Of course, she would.*

He told her of the East Broadway tenement he shared with his parents and two sisters. Of dropping out of school at fourteen to work as a dishwasher at a semi-fancy midtown restaurant. To help his parents make ends meet, the gap between their sweatshop wages and the family's living expenses often being Hudson-River-wide.

Of being taken under the wing of the restaurant's head chef, a proud Afro-Frenchman— "like Dumas!" he'd proclaim—who was exiled from his home country for a never-spoken crime. Of being promoted from dishwasher to apprentice cook, no longer cleaning dirty pots and pans but dirtying them via sliced vegetables and meats and mixed sauces.

Here is alchemy, he had thought, having just learned the word from the *Weird Tales* magazines he read during his breaks. The most unexceptional ingredients—say, oxtail, onions, carrots from the local food stall—could be transformed into the most remarkably delicious dishes. What could be more magical than that?

Once he knew such knowledge existed, his need to learn was relentless, as was his rise up the kitchen hierarchy. Within a couple of years, from apprentice to junior cook to *sous chef* ...

"And then to head chef, right?" Molly said, nodding along to his story.

"No, I never made it. I quit before then."

"What? Why?"

"I got bored."

Which, he informed her immediately afterward, simplified his reasoning. He had a plan. Once he had sponged up everything a restaurant could teach him, he'd quit and start at the bottom at a grander restaurant and begin the sponging process again. It worked like a charm, though it necessitated a decade and a half of sixteen-hour workdays, falling asleep on subway cars if not on kitchen floors, and a laundry list of abortive relationships.

Still, by his thirty-first birthday, the day after Pearl Harbor, when he'd volunteered for the military and gotten rejected due to a childhood ear operation, he had built up a culinary resume impressive enough to get him through the gilded swinging doors at the French restaurant atop Rockefeller Center.

He had a short break before his position started and decided to liquidate his meager savings for the first real vacation of his life. He had only one desire: to eat the best French food he could find, in order to prepare for his new job. Since Paris was out—too expensive, too Nazi-controlled—Montreal was the best alternative, and he enjoyed two idyllic weeks there.

He window-shopped along the Rue St-Paul, marveled at the city's own Notre Dame Basilica, hiked in the Laurentian Mountains. Most of all, he ate—at sidewalk stands, mid-priced eateries, and even two-century-old establishments like the L'Auberge Saint-Gabriel. He discovered what he had long suspected and found yet again …

"You saw the beauty behind the everyday," Molly finished for him.

"Yes, I did," John said and laughed. He had repeated the axiom enough, maybe more than enough, and he understood it could, to cynics, sound like a clichéd Hallmark Card.

But he never felt that way about the phrase, and he suspected neither did Molly. To him, it was undeniable truth. Most people didn't see the beauty behind the everyday, didn't enjoy the simple pleasures in life, didn't stop and smell the roses … and just because these phrases were considered platitudes didn't make them any less true. For you could belittle truth, lambaste it, deny its existence, but truth would always still be there, as unconcerned as the inexorably flowing Mississippi.

"Halfway through my trip in Montreal," he said, "I realized I didn't need to be *in* Montreal to feel great about myself and my surroundings. I didn't need to shop at the Jean-Talon Market when any American supermarket would do since, to the people who live there, that was *their* supermarket. It was just a change of perspective, you know?"

"I think I know what you mean," Molly said, but her left raised eyebrow was skeptical. "I just have a hard time wrapping my mind around the fact that where we're at now is as, for lack of a better word, *romantic* as a … I don't know, a beachside bungalow in Bora Bora."

"It's not. It's *more* romantic, especially with the present company."

He knew the line was corny, like something from a rejected B-movie script. But her reaction, an acknowledging but shy smile, was unparalleled enchantment and more than enough confirmation of his stated belief.

He knew it was the summer of 1961 and that he was in a normal American house, standing inside a normal American kitchen. Vinyl counters and flooring, Frigidaire fridge, General Electric range, RCA radio delivering light music. The world outside was interstate highways, transoceanic telegraph wires, and TWA flights to Europe and South America. He knew there were no more blank spaces on maps, and there were no wizards in towers or serpents in the seas. Cold logic and all its metastasized forms—supersonic jets, Russian spy satellites, atomic bombs—had obliterated all the magic of the world.

But John knew that belief was wrong. Magic did still exist, even, maybe especially, in the most outwardly colorless of places. In the house he was in now. The kind of magic that would've made the never-existent Merlin green with envy. The magic of the mind and the soul and the lives of ordinary people. *Real* magic.

He never made the mistake of so many of his contemporaries in thinking the present was drab or was somehow a pale imitation of a more glorious, romantic past. Just as the everyday settings of life were not everyday at all, so too was the present not colorless. It was 1961 Mississippi, true, but John had no doubt, in some future year—2061, 3061 maybe—this time and place would be as extraordinary as Renaissance Florence under the House of the Medici.

His preparing dinner wasn't an isolated action but just the latest incarnation in a never-ending stream of cooked meals throughout human history, from every culture and location of the world, back to the prehistory of an open fire in the Great Rift Valley. And each occurrence had its own unique, beautiful story.

He could almost see those people, the meal preparers of yesterday or yesteryear or even yester-millennium, and if he were to stop his own activities and close his eyes, he was sure he could hear them too. These people no different from his own being, no matter how dissimilar their skin colors or cultures or epochs were. He and they were the same, as all humanity was the same, from the modern world to the mists of antiquity.

The Egyptian ferryman aboard his boat sharing his dinner of bread and scallions with the reed cutter's daughter, the setting sunlight split by the great pyramids on the horizon. The Polynesian couple grilling prawns on some unspoiled tropical paradise, centuries before the arrival of Europeans and colonization and disease. The 19th-century gaucho, herding his stock on the southern edge of the world, Argentine Patagonia, his loneliness only alleviated by his monthly visits to the town's inn, where he was served dinner by the innkeeper's alluring wife.

All these meals were just snapshots of love among common men and women. Loves that were not unlike Romeo and Juliet's or Launcelot and Guinevere's or any of the other love stories immortalized in print or performance. Except the love stories of common folk were always forgotten by the passage of time.

But John knew the best love stories were the ones that were never told. For no medium—no book, no poem, no play or movie—could ever tell a love story in its entirety, its full span and depth, from the exhilarating beginning to the tragic ending of all love stories. He didn't mind if his life was forgotten—it had never occurred to him to *want* to be remembered—as long as he had truly lived, and to live life without experiencing one great love story was to not live at all.

Which was why this moment, in this outwardly undistinguished house, was so magic-suffused. He knew he and the woman beside him had begun one such love story together. Molly Valle, a woman he hadn't known two weeks earlier, a woman he hadn't even kissed.

Yet he knew. He knew.

"What's funny?" she asked beside him, and he realized he had been smiling.

John returned to the world then, as he often had as a daydreaming kid. But this time, he had returned to a reality that was better than his dreams.

"Everything, I guess." He placed the mystery dish into the oven and set the temperature and timer. "This is going to take about forty-five minutes."

He followed her into the backyard where she showcased her beds of petunias, zinnias, and caladiums—the flowers she had to name in advance since he couldn't tell a rose from a carnation to save his life. As she spoke, he tried his hardest to concentrate on what she was pointing at and not the brown arm doing the pointing or the body, seemingly honey-coated by the setting sun, that the arm was attached to.

Afterward, she took him through a tour of the house itself. The living room, the single bathroom, and, without entering, the two bedrooms. The house was small, but, unlike the transitory dwellings he had lived in for God knew how long, it had a wonderful singularity and permanence. It was Molly Valle's *home* through and through, with each loving touch as full of her as the cells in her body.

The eclectic selection of books on her shelves (*Peyton Place; I, the Jury;* Churchill's *Second World War*); the self-created abstract paintings on her walls ("My college art teacher was an overly enthusiastic devotee of Duchamp"); the giant, kitschy pink-flamingo lamp ("Saw that sucker at a crafts store in Miami and knew I had to have him") …

He walked beside her, in front of her, behind her. He tried not to be overwhelmed by her fragrance and sheer presence. Yet, beyond the near-overwhelming desire for Molly Valle, he felt something else. It was as if the hands of some internal clock had long been off-kilter and had, at last, rearranged themselves into the correct positions.

Walking in this small house, John felt freer than he had ever felt in his entire life. Freer than he had felt while camping in the Laurentian Mountains, when his view was unobscured by city lights and he could at night, while lying on the damp grass, seemingly look past the hundred billion stars of the Milky Way to the very edge of the expanding universe.

Yes, he felt freer now, inside this house and its walls. He normally loathed walls. Physical barriers that became mental ones for most people, shutting out the view of the outside world—the world of dreams, travel, and adventure. The walls of a home were even worse. Homes were shackles that could've constrained Houdini.

But he didn't feel that way now. *That's the strange thing about love. It skews all of your perceptions.* And he knew what he was feeling was love. Of that, he had no doubt. Furthermore, the knowledge was accented with not the slightest fear but with an excitement bordering on hysteria.

"So, that's all she wrote," Molly said as the tour ended in the living room and they sat down, she on the love seat, he on an adjacent chair, the coffee table between them. "What do you think?"

"I think this is what they would call the cat's meow back in the day. Something my sisters would've dreamed about, growing up crammed in that tiny apartment."

"Something that your sisters dreamed about, but not you, right?"

John noted her smile and the serious nature of the question beneath its surface humor. He started to say one thing but then realized that wasn't what he wanted to say. He didn't know what to say, and he finally decided on that truth: "I don't know."

"Your sisters aren't like you, right? Adventurous?"

"I wouldn't call myself that. I guess, from an early age, I just wanted to see new things in life. I thought that was how I always would be."

She nodded, the lamp beside her casting a warm amber glow on her face, the contours of which seemed, for a second, like gently sloping sand dunes. He wanted to explore that face—every line, every dip and rise—like a cartographer mapping every exotic locale known to man.

"And I wouldn't call my sisters unadventurous," he told her. "They just like security."

Molly nodded, but her eyes swept across her living room, as if assessing it for the first time. Then she said quietly, "Security is overrated."

"Maybe, but not for everyone," he said after a moment, thinking about the security he had always feared and run away from. The security that, symbolized by this ordinary suburban house, now seemed unexpectedly wonderful, even sublime.

"If you had grown up like we had," he continued, "security sometimes seems wonderful."

"Maybe, but I grew up pretty much like now," Molly said. "Solidly, boringly middle-class, you could say. I don't know why, but I chose security over everything else too."

He thought about her actions at the diner, the only person who had done anything. He thought about the divorce he knew she had but never talked about.

No, Molly Valle, you didn't choose security at all.

He looked at her sitting there, middle-aged and, because of all the lived experiences that age had afforded her, so luminously beautiful. This knowledge suddenly made him realize that, for the first time in his life, he envied someone else. He who had never wished to trade one second of his life with anyone else's.

He found that he envied Molly's ex-husband, whoever the fool might've been. The man who had been married to her, who therefore had the whole world and everything in it, but who had then so blindly and so stupidly—stupidity bordering the farthest reaches of insanity—thrown everything away.

"You know, when I look at this house, this comfortable house," John found himself saying, "I wonder if I maybe chose my life without enough concern for security."

"Just like I feel I've erred too much on the side of caution."

He nodded and stood up. "You know what this means, don't you?"

"What?" she asked and smiled, the smile both hesitant and expectant.

"We can meet in the middle."

He stepped toward her, and she stood up. He wrapped his arms around her, feeling her body for the first time—the warmth, the solidity, the rightness of it. Then, right before their lips met, the timer in the kitchen rang, sounding like the loudest air-raid siren in the known world.

CHAPTER 15

MOLLY

The timer going off felt like, in Molly's mind, the loudest wail from the most annoying baby in the world. Yet it merely announced that John's dish, whatever it was, was ready—the dinner that was the ostensible reason for his being there. John, who was still holding her with his face an inch from hers.

No, just leave it alone and kiss me.

But then he smiled and said, "Dinner's ready," and disengaged his arms—those thick, wonderful arms—from around her body, turned, and walked toward the kitchen. Molly watched him go, still swimming in his scent—a bit of aftershave and something hard to define yet thoroughly masculine—her body rigid, her mind exploding with one word: *No.*

He disappeared into the kitchen. She heard him turn off the timer, and then he returned. Still smiling. Walking back to her.

"We can always heat it up later," he said.

Molly laughed then, laughed hard, but that laugh was cut off as John's lips pressed against hers, and they were kissing. Devouring yet oddly symmetrically perfect kisses as if her lips were made only for his. Kisses that she felt on her lips, her face, her neck, her body, all the way down to the toenails she'd painstakingly painted that morning.

She heard herself moan.

"Come on"—the command came, and she didn't even know who had said it.

John was in her bedroom, and she didn't even know how they got there. Teleportation maybe. They were kissing in her bedroom, and she suddenly felt the wetness between her legs. The sensation was so rare and so unexpected, she laughed in surprise and with a relief so bottomless, she felt she could dive happily to the center of the world.

"Yes?" John inquired, her laughing having broken their kiss.

"Nothing," she said, finding it hard to talk, so euphoric was she. "It's just that this—this is my bedroom." And she laughed again.

He nodded as if he understood her gibberish. Maybe he did. No, she *knew* he did.

The bedroom that had never entertained any other body but her own. She'd purchased her house after her divorce, and had, even at that dispiriting time, entertained thoughts of sharing the space eventually with a new man. How long ago was that moment? She knew but didn't want to remember it or its shameful naïveté.

So many years alone in this bedroom, with its Georgia O'Keeffe's *Black Hills with Cedar* print, subdued drum lampshades, the green and brown motif. She had come to terms with her loneliness, as if it were a second, mocking presence in this room, as solid as a piece of immovable furniture.

Now, that loneliness had vanished without a trace, and in its place was John Pressman. It was as if all the stories contained within *One Thousand and One Arabian Nights* spilled out into glorious, riotous reality in this previously most humdrum place in the world.

She was naked. How all her clothes came off, she didn't remember, whether by his hands or her own. She was naked, and so was John. Or, at least, he was in the process of getting naked, taking off his shirt and exposing his bare, wonderful torso. No undershirt for this primordial man. But a man's nakedness was different from a woman's, wasn't it?

How many years? How many years have passed since I last stood in my birthday suit before a man?

She didn't remember, but the number she did know was eleven. Eleven pounds lighter was what she'd been the last time someone saw her naked. Eleven pounds that had slowly but doggedly appeared on the bathroom scale. Eleven pounds that hadn't been distributed where she'd wanted them distributed—her breasts, her too-thin calves—but where she most decidedly didn't want. Places where gravity, the middle-aged woman's nemesis, could most easily work its dark deeds. Not to mention the accumulated nicks that went with living forty-eight hard years on the planet.

Her lean, comparatively flawless twenty-something self was long in the past and—she hated admitting this to herself—so was a great deal of her former confidence. What replaced them was a single, stu-pid question, and even knowing its stupidity did not lessen its sting. *How could she meet an attractive man who would also find* her *attrac-tive?* Especially a man as singularly attractive as John Pressman? A man who had, no doubt, enjoyed far more beautiful women in New York City and indeed had Bethanee, a striking woman just entering her prime, practically salivating over him back at the college?

But then John said a single word, a single truth, that exposed all those insecure thoughts in her mind as what they were: sheer insan-ity. "Beautiful," he said to her, and then stepping back, as if to admire a sculpture in toto, he said the word again.

"Beautiful."

She smiled and flushed, his gaze a corporeal warmth, like gentle, invisible hands caressing each part of her body. She stood naked in front of him, and in a miraculous instant, her self-consciousness vanished.

In place of insecurity and doubt were a new-found pride and a blindingly obvious understanding. She *was* beautiful. Not despite her so-called flaws but *because* of them—those scrapes and life experiences that made her body like no other woman's. The beauty that wasn't ephemeral or society-dictated but the *real* beauty that cut across generations, across all cultures, from the beginning of humankind. The beauty that was painted in Paleolithic caves and carved in ancient Venus statuettes, those wonderful figurines of all shapes and sizes, individualized and gorgeous precisely because of that individuality. What cavemen had known, modern men had forgotten, and sadly, modern women too.

Molly realized that she herself had forgotten. But not anymore. For now, she witnessed the truth of her beauty reflected back at her through John's eyes—the twin blue mirrors that showcased, to paraphrase Virginia Woolf's immortal phrase, her splendor at twice its power.

But two can play this game. A delicious thrill went through her as he took off the last of his clothes and she could survey him as he had her moments earlier.

Genuine—that was the word that came to her. His body was genuine. Strong with naturally wide shoulders and thick arms—and a middle that would never fit inside Montgomery Clift's jeans. But then John didn't need to. He was not from the Hollywood assembly line, was no Cary Grant or Errol Flynn or Rock Hudson, men made dashing by acting coaches and molded to play factory workers, farmhands, and ranchers. But they were only pretending, whereas John, just by being himself, looked like the real thing and not its approximation.

His was not a body that came from lifting shiny weights in a Jack LaLanne health club but from heaving cast-iron pots and pans in tight spaces near open flames. A body that came from living, not playacting. A body that held itself to nobody's standard but its own and was thus unburdened by barriers to authenticity.

This attitude has served him well for fifty years, Molly thought, looking at him, ogling him even. And she guessed it would continue to do so through the next twenty, thirty, forty years that he had left. The genuineness of his body. No, of his entire being, full stop.

They were making love, this genuine body of his with hers, now also accepting of its own genuineness and therefore its own beauty unbounded. Body parts of his that should not be used for sex according to polite society, but which Molly very much knew from her recent Kinsey readings *were* used, though she never had with any man until this exquisite moment. His hands, his lips, his *tongue* …

She panted and panted, then it came, all-powerful and pleasurable, like an aria so perfect and extended, it was almost painful. She cried out, her whole body shuddering, her eyes squeezed shut, and then his head was no longer between her legs but was kissing her full on her mouth, her tongue tasting his tongue and her own scent, wholly exotic despite its own familiarity. Something new, something new here.

The crest came and went, and in its wake, she knew it had been more powerful than any she'd felt as a young woman. She reflected then how silly she'd been once, thinking that, after crossing the forty-year mark, sex was only a source of pleasure for the young.

"Oh, God, John," Molly managed to say as his lips fell away from hers. As she opened her eyes, he entered her for the first time, and despite his gentle motion, it felt invading and painful—but only for a split-second. Then, as he moved his hips in sync with hers, it became as natural and integral as a part of her own body, her arm, her leg, her heart.

Again, she thought, in absolute wonder: *I am in the same place that I'm always in every night.* It was as if she'd gone to the ends of the Earth in search of adventure, past poison-dart-blowing tribes and across mighty, caiman-infested rivers, only to see, overgrown with roots from a towering Amazonian tree, her own house with its thirty-year fixed mortgage.

At forty-eight years of age, in this most outwardly prosaic of locations, she discarded the man-made shackles that bound middle-aged women to the sexually invisible role. If she had her hands free, she'd do what she'd seen beatniks do in magazine photos: throw up two defiant middle fingers, at the male universe that had denied her *this* for so long.

For now, though, she was sex incarnate, and her hands had far better things to do. She was under John, then above him, then beside him, then standing in front of him, then against the wall, against the bed, against the floorboard. Moving in sync like one half of a perfectly moist, organic machine.

The years fell away, but she felt not so much young as ageless and all-powerful. All parts of her indeed enjoyed the thrusts and licks and kisses so much more than when she had been young. Making love that had none of the uncomprehending vacuity or clumsy over-excitement of youth.

It felt familiar yet, with John Pressman, wholly novel. This was two people with the experience of age and knowledge to know their socially deemed imperfect bodies were in actuality perfect bodies. Self-confident bodies that were very much engaged in the act of self-confident fucking.

Her first orgasm was soon succeeded by another, then another, then she lost count. What she vaguely became aware of, like a weak lighthouse beam through the heavy mist of pleasure, was John enjoying the moment as much as she, with his moans and breathless whispers in her ear, the words unintelligible but their meaning still manifest.

She didn't know how long they went at it like that, but it felt like a long, long time—but in a good way. She liked possessing a man so totally, just as she liked being totally possessed by a man. Not only her body and mind and soul but her entire life, her past, her everything.

Inside her mind, she felt increasingly adrift, as if their lovemaking had reached a realm that transcended the physical body. She saw herself float above her body, past her ceiling, through her roof, and higher and higher, the entire world pulsating and alive with sensations. Even these receded as she floated above her town, the pinpoints of the shop windows and car headlights downtown, then she was even higher, above the mighty Mississippi.

Just when she wondered if she would just continue gliding up, to the stratosphere and beyond, she found herself drifting down again, though whether this action took a minute or an hour, she had no clue. Time meant nothing here, and so it was neither day nor night—nor, for that matter, the present day, year, or decade.

She was seeing a ten-year-old girl, skin made tawny by the invisible summer sun, sitting alone on a grassy bluff overlooking the river. She was crying to herself, and Molly knew, as plainly as she felt the unperfumed breeze against her face, what the reason was. The girl felt her whole life would be one of loneliness, and so she cried.

Molly wanted to hug the young girl close, stroke her black hair and tell her that loneliness, while unpleasant, was endurable. Not once, though, did she consider telling the girl that she was wrong for that reassurance would be a lie, wouldn't it be? She was, after all, *her*, and in the intervening four decades, the girl's prescience had been proven right. Loneliness had indeed been the condition—would *always* be the condition—of Molly's life, of being misunderstood and neglected by others, even amidst a crowd and friends and, for a few years, a husband.

But then a boy, maybe a year or two older than ten-year-old Molly, walked past forty-eight-year-old Molly. He had thick blond hair and a small scar on his chin and, though not yet a teenager, had already developed a late-teenager's husky build.

Why are you crying? the boy asked the girl, and adult Molly could not so much hear his words as sense them.

I dreamed I was going to be alone all my life, the girl said, looking up.

Why, nobody would marry you?

No, I will get married, many years from now. But I was still alone, and then I got divorced. Will always be alone.

The boy thought a second then took her hand. How could you be alone, he told the girl, when I'll be right there with you your whole life?

The girl smiled, not a radiant smile but a hesitant one, as if she were grappling with the truth of the boy's assertion. Then she nodded and stood up.

You promise? she asked the boy.

Of course, he said and wiped the tears from her eyes. And together, the girl and the boy, hand in hand, walked away from adult Molly.

Her gaze followed them, but they were no longer near the river.

They were nowhere in particular and everywhere at once. Sitting next to each other in chemistry class as teenagers, exchanging notes when the teacher had his back turned. Going to prom together. Both losing their virginity to the other the summer after high school. Her teaching-training program at the local college in tandem with his education at a culinary school in Jackson, pining for each other during the week, smothering each other's faces with kisses on the weekends.

School ended, and she became a teacher and he a chef at a downtown French restaurant. They married. Molly's mother was there and so was her father, still wonderfully alive, and John—for who else could it have been but John—had invited his parents and sisters. John, looking lean in his rented tuxedo, in his mid-twenties, as handsome as could be. But, Molly reflected, no more handsome than his admittedly heftier self a quarter-century later.

The young couple honeymooned in Miami then, with the Overseas Highway still decades in the future, took a languid ferry out to Key West, where they wore flowery clothes and rode rusty beach cruisers around the island.

Five years after returning to Mississippi, they had a son whom they named Paul, so achingly beautiful and fragile, and together they spent restless nights thinking how they could protect him in this fallen world. But their worries thankfully proved unfounded as Paul, with his mom's olive skin and his dad's dark blond hair, grew up healthy and strong. Which was why he, at sixteen, was off to summer camp in Natchez, allowing his parents a two-week rest and another chance at adventure.

John Pressman and Molly Valle Pressman, husband and wife, rollicking in their small but perfect house on a summer night in 1961. Making love in the dark as vigorously as they had when they were thirty, twenty-one, eighteen …

Molly cried out as she climaxed again, both the Molly of reality and the Molly in her mind. She must've been the same person since John held her. John, who had been with her all her life. How could he not have been when she felt nothing but an aching closeness to him, this man who knew her better than anyone else in the world, better than even she knew herself? How could he not have been with her all these decades?

Those memories of her solitary existence—they could be nothing but melancholy dreams. They couldn't have contained the truth, could they? That somehow, in a random meeting at a diner just two weeks earlier, she'd found, like in a fanciful fairy tale, her knight in shining armor. No, that event couldn't have happened. That would be too outrageous, too unbelievable.

But then John kissed her again, and she knew it didn't matter. Memories were powerful and real, but this moment was even more so. She was with John *now*, and with it came a realization so powerful and pure, it brought tears to her eyes. Molly knew that she would, at forty-eight years, six months, and three days of age, never be alone again.

"Why are you crying?" he asked, his handsome face wetly bright even in the dark.

"I'm just so happy I've found you," she told him and laughed through her tears.

"Likewise, my lady."

He kissed her lips again. Then, lowering his head, he kissed her neck, her breasts, her belly, and stopped kissing and began licking six inches below that.

CHAPTER 16

JOHN

When he woke, it was still dark. For a few moments, he was unsure where he was, the silvery shapes of some delightful dream fading. He tried to recall what the dream had been about, but then he heard her breathing beside him and whatever desire he'd had to remember instantly vanished. He knew he was experiencing one of those very rare moments that only came maybe a couple of times in a human lifespan, when a person awoke from an ecstatic dream to find an even more joyful reality.

John Pressman, naked, his skin still sticky from his Olympian exertions, turned toward Molly Valle sleeping beside him. She was also nude and was sleeping on her stomach. He contemplated the plane of her back dipping to the small of her back before climbing up the slope of her butt. This magnificent landscape was accentuated by the patina of her own sweat, and, while she breathed, her back rose and fell like a graceful wave on the most beautiful sea in the world. The extraordinary body that held the even more extraordinary mind and soul.

My Molly. The two words were spellbinding in their simplicity and in their totality of bliss. *My Molly.* He still had the taste of her in his mouth.

He felt himself stir downstairs and reached out to her but then stopped himself. *No, let her sleep.* She deserved it, as did he.

He turned onto his back again and tried to fall asleep. But he knew he couldn't. He thought about what had happened just a couple of hours earlier and couldn't quite grasp it. She on top of him, grinding him, below him, crying out, laughing … being with Molly had been like the discovery of the first time. Except that wasn't quite right for his first time was a fumbling, anxious, unsatisfying affair.

No, being with Molly was what young people *imagined* their first time as being: life-altering and achingly perfect. He was dazzled. Dazzled, dazzled, dazzled.

Molly was the first woman he had been with who had wholly given in to and enjoyed the act. He had been with many women whom society deemed more adventurous, the bohemian artists of Greenwich Village, where he'd once lived, or the Upper East Side socialites who'd fancied his cooking and sometimes much more.

Something held those women back. They were embarrassed by their own smell or taste or wants or needs. Maybe afraid of what polite society, indoctrinated by Procter & Gamble and *Father Knows Best*, always labeled women who enjoyed the sex act so freely: the shrews or, worse, the sluts. To fight against these falsehoods, though, one needed to be able to see past the present-day and very male-oriented distortion lens to the underlying truth.

Beyond question, Molly Valle could do this. A woman whose surface appearance, eyeglasses and conservative clothes, fit the schoolmarm stereotype to a T. Yet she had sloughed off that exterior and society's restrictions as effortlessly as she had her clothes, and during their lovemaking, she had not only kept up with him but often passed ahead of him. With other women, he had seen the embers of passion but never the flame. Tonight, he had witnessed the bonfire.

He was so thankful he was able to see that spirit, to experience it firsthand, for he guessed Molly's spirit hadn't come out in a long, long time. Not because she was repressed—God knew, she wasn't in the least bit—but rather because her passion was undirected. It was as if she had surveyed the land of men and found it most grievously wanting.

Molly Valle, the most nonjudgmental person he had ever known, nonetheless seemed to sense the shallowness and unfitness of most men. Sensed it on a deep, almost cellular level. How, by not seeing her passionate inner self—in essence, not seeing *her*—most men had automatically made themselves unworthy of that passion. Her rejection of them wasn't borne out of snobbery but a crystalline understanding of reality.

How stupid men are.

John couldn't help but experience a childlike burst of pride. Pride—one of the seven deadly sins, true, but he felt it all the same. The goddess of sex that most men had fantasized about since their teenage years wasn't to be found in some red-light district of town or in an illicit magazine but was actually standing right next to them at work, at the library, at the coffee shop. And they were too blind to see it!

They had all missed Molly Valle, the rose that—no, not the rose. What was the state flower of Mississippi? The magnolia, he remembered vaguely. Yes, the magnolia. She was the magnolia that bloomed unseen. Except *he* had seen it.

I had a good life. John took a quick glance at her sleeping beside him. *Now, I will have a great life.*

Except that wasn't quite right. No, he realized that his past life, his past lonely life, hadn't been good but perfect. For every single event in that life had pushed him unwaveringly closer and closer to her. Every failure, every crumbling relationship, every breakup in the cold rain or amidst hot tears—everything had been to place him at that diner two weeks ago. To bring him to the *now*—sleeping on her bed, this stunning, intelligent woman next to him.

All his life, he had dreamt of her, either consciously or subconsciously, and this woman had materialized in the flesh. Looking back, he wondered if the plan had been too perfect for it to be mere coincidence. Fate or whatever could substitute for fate had slowly moved him toward her. Such bliss, such consummation of all his dreams, couldn't have come from some random, chance encounter, could it have?

He doubted it—or did he? In his lifetime, he had seen enough injustice to know the world was cold and remorseless and didn't care one fig about the happiness of people. He tried to live a good life and devote that life to helping others, but he never thought the world would reward him for his efforts. Such a thought would be the ultimate in self-deluding self-aggrandizement, for why would the world care one iota about *him*?

Now, however, he wondered if he had been wrong. Now, he thought that maybe, just maybe, if you lived a good life, the universe—this cold, cold world—might just reward you. And he did feel rewarded—rewarded beyond all the gold in the Aztec capital of Tenochtitlan.

He took one last, discreet glance at Molly's naked back, the beauty of it and of her, and then turning away, he forced his eyes closed. As he drifted back to sleep, however, he realized something new, and he almost laughed aloud.

For the first time past the age of thirty-five, he realized he didn't want to enjoy his sleep anymore. Like a kid before Christmas morning, he wanted to wake up as soon as possible.

Still dwelling on this happy image, John Pressman of New York fell asleep beside Molly Valle of Mississippi on one summer night in 1961.

CHAPTER 17

MOLLY

She awoke with her eyes still closed. From a dream—that much she knew. But *which* dream? She had two. The one where he had been always there for her, since they were children, or the other one, where he was nearing fifty-one and was beneath her, atop her, inside her?

When she finally opened her eyes and saw her own ceiling, she knew which one had been real. As if in confirmation, she felt the soreness between her legs. So *that* dream had been real, after all. Yes, *that* had been very, very real. She felt a smile stretch her cheeks.

Although Molly heard John sleeping beside her, she didn't turn her head or even move quite yet. Instead, she luxuriated in the alpenglow of the fabulously fucked. All the images flooded back to her then. His sweat-glistening face in the dark, his muscular shoulders, his perfectly timed thrusts, and, most of all, his unselfishness in pleasuring her, pleasuring her, pleasuring her …

In recalling those images, she suddenly felt wetness with her soreness, and her right arm, as if by its own volition, reached for him. She stopped it just in time. No, let him sleep. He—*it*—deserved a week's worth of rest after last night. *A month's worth maybe.* She nearly laughed out loud.

But she did finally turn toward him and, throwing all caution to the wind, thought, *My man.* This person she hadn't even known a month ago, two weeks ago. The other dream of meeting John when he was a boy—that, she knew, wasn't true. John Pressman was a Yankee, a New Yorker even, through and through. Yet, in fundamental ways, he wasn't a New Yorker at all. He didn't seem rooted to any particular place or time. Besides, geographic and temporal considerations distracted from the essential truth: she would never be alone again.

She looked at his face, his lined, well-lived face. *You were right.* This perfect moment, in her once-desolate bedroom, was John's belief at its apotheosis. She realized she wouldn't have believed it before—that, in the most hopelessly constricted of places, you could find the fulfillment to all your dreams of adventure and romance. No, she wouldn't have believed it. Not twenty years ago, not ten years ago, not a year ago.

She had to reach forty-eight years of age to realize the truth and to internalize it. Forty-eight long years of groping in the dark. How silly she felt now and how blessed. *Better late than never*—another cliché that she had frequently brushed past and never considered. How true that cliché also was, and how damn good it all felt.

Soon, John would wake up and leave her, at least for the day, to right one injustice in a world chockful of injustices. In imagining his day, Molly understood what she was going to do for the rest of her life. The world was so wrong, so disastrously cruel, and in so many ways, it became clear to her that she would try to right it somehow, even in the minuscule measure that a single human being could influence.

She would no longer build a shaky wall around herself like she had before or be surprised at being loathed by a young black woman whom she hardly knew. She wanted to help end that peculiar injustice in her town, then her state, then the entire region around her state, and, if that miracle were to come before her death by old age, she would continue onward to other injustices, which seemed like viruses overwhelming the healthy body of the world.

She even had a partner in crime, a man whose wonderful mysteries she would also need a lifetime to unravel, and she was so looking forward to this task.

Molly leaned forward to the sleeping form beside her for a kiss but, fearing he would awaken, instead slowly traced the one-inch scar on his chin with her tongue. Exploring it like a Venetian merchant of a millennium past, map and torch in hand, lost off the Silk Road but discovering an uncharted Central Asian ravine filled with lost treasure.

She licked his salty skin, remnants of last night's exertions, and breathed in his musky, masculine scent, her eyes closed, her ears registering nothing, but her other three senses—touch, taste, smell—so heightened, she almost couldn't stand it.

When her tongue reached the end of the scar—the passage whether measured in seconds or eons, she didn't know—and she opened her eyes, she saw that John had come awake and was staring at her. She drew back and smiled an embarrassed smile, which he returned.

"Hi," he said.

"Hi," she said.

They were both quiet for a moment, but, in that silence, everything was said. What she offered next seemed to be nothing but punctuation to that all-meaningful stillness.

"I love you."

"Me too," he said.

They laughed then, raucous, freewheeling laughter in the once-silent room where her dreams had come to die, now made real and glorious by this son of New York. She snorted, became slightly mortified, and snorted even harder.

"What?" John asked,

"I don't know why, but I was—I was thinking, just now, of *Richard III*."

He thought just a split-second before replying, "'Made glorious summer by the sun of York'? You're saying I'm Richard III?"

"Heavens no," she said, not surprised that he could quote Shakespeare. "He was a grade-A bastard."

When the second round of laughter had petered out, he asked her, "You hungry?"

"Famished."

He stood up, exposing his imperfectly perfect body in all its glory.

"Stay right here," he told her, "I'll be back with breakfast in ten minutes."

"Not on your life, sir," Molly said. "I shall assist you."

She jumped out of the bed as naked and free as Eve before the bitten apple, forty-eight years, six months, and four days old—the most beautiful she had ever felt in her life.

CHAPTER 18

THE PRESENT
RC

The story should've ended right there, with the forty-eight-year-old Molly Valle, strong in body and mind, rising like a fabled phoenix from the ashy ennui of her middle years, to begin the rest of her life with the love of her life. A happily-ever-after moment, if there ever was one.

If this were a novel, the reader would close the book with a satisfied sigh, and if this were a play, the stage curtains would begin to gently fall. Except reality doesn't work in such a manner, and I am again struck by the unfairness of life. It never ends when it should but always at the most inconvenient times.

It is summer still, but this summer is separated from the earlier one by over a thousand miles and a half-century. It is the present, and I am in Molly Valle's apartment in southern California. The living room surprisingly looks the same as it did when I first saw it thirty years ago. The same array of photos, the same overstuffed bookshelves, the same culturally diverse artifacts. The immutable, lived-in quality of the place brings me comfort, especially since the two people here have changed so much.

I am no longer a fifteen-year-old nicknamed RC, a dreamy boy with visions of a grand future as a rich and famous novelist married to a brilliant, Playboy-bunny-looking woman. No, I am a forty-four-year-old high school English teacher, a failed writer, and still single.

In all honesty, I've failed at everything I've ever touched, but in one of those quirks of fate, my failures allowed me all summer to sit by Molly and hear her story. She read one of my published stories in a literary magazine and believed I could write the story. *Her* story. And I very much want to hear it, but she is asleep. She is asleep a lot these days.

The vibrant middle-aged lady was a half-century in the past, and the spry seventy-three-year-old woman I first met was three decades back.

She let me have a set of keys when she began telling her story a week ago, and I let myself in every day at noon. She was asleep when I came in today, confined to her electric wheelchair in the living room, her white hair draping her lined face. The face that John Pressman fell in love with, the face that is still beautiful.

Beautiful and even healthy until your gaze shifts a few inches downward. Then you see the blanket covering her shoulders poke out in disturbingly sharp angles, symptoms of a body slowly defeated by age and now afflicted with disease. This is another aspect of life—the devastating endgame of all people's fates.

So I sit on a La-Z-Boy and wait for Molly, just ten feet away, to wake up. I turn over in my mind the remarkable love story she's been telling me, made even more remarkable by the fact it is being told by one half of the real-life couple.

Half, I think and feel a mounting dread.

Among all the photos in the apartment, I can only see one of John Pressman—the same one I first spied when I was a teenager. The photo where he looks fifty, the same age he was when he met Molly. Although I never asked her, I know this is the only one she has of him. Every night, back in my own apartment, I want to Google him, but I don't. I want Molly to tell me the full story, you see. This story I don't fully understand.

It's like this: If I close my eyes, I can almost see the sweltering '60s Mississippi of the tale. But the reality of that story and my present reality are too wide apart. I am a great lover of stories and even, in my own inadequate way, a creator of them too.

But I've always felt stories are merely vessels that take you out of your humdrum reality. They are escapism and nothing more. But Molly told me her story isn't escapist but relevant to my own life. On this point, I just don't feel it, this story contained in my tape recorder.

Except my tape recorder isn't actually a tape recorder. It's the voice memos app on my iPhone, a gadget that would've been wizardry back when Molly Valle was my age. The days of Jim Crow are long and forever gone. I fear that Molly's story, while beautiful, has no more relevance to my day than room-sized computers, extra-large automobile tailfins, and beehive hairdos. As much as I want to believe that adventure lies beneath the everyday—John Pressman's refrain—I also know that, when I leave Molly's apartment this evening, I will get into my seven-year-old Hyundai and drive home to my small, lonely apartment in Los Angeles.

Where is the magic in rush-hour traffic on the 405 Freeway?

No, life has no soundtrack, just the daily grind occasionally alleviated by short-lived bursts of happiness—a vacation, the birth of a child, retirement. This is my life and the life of everyone I know—all my friends, all my family members, everyone with whom I have more than a passing acquaintance. I've spent nearly forty-five years on this planet, and the majority of those years—my adult years, my reality-based years—have shown me that the adventure Molly and John had no longer exists. This is why I so want Molly to wake up and tell me that I'm wrong.

But she is still asleep, and I get up to head to the kitchen to get a glass of water. As I pass her, however, I stop and study her sleeping form. Her body is gone, and she is dependent on others—a nurse comes by nightly—but within her sparrow-brittle frame still dwells the indomitable woman John Pressman loved. In discerning this fact, I feel a kinship with this man whom I've never met. He and I could both see Molly Valle for who she is—a real wonder, kind and smart and brave, a beautiful woman warrior minus the breastplate.

I smile at this image, but then the smile falters as I once again contemplate how unjust life is. You see, I grew to love her too in many ways. But Molly and I are separated not by one generation but two, she of the World War II generation and I, born in the early 1970s, solidly of the Generation X mold.

When I return to the living room with my glass of water, I find Molly awake and looking at me. Her body is wrecked, but her brown eyes are sharp.

"My knight," she says and smiles. Her voice is weak but clearer than yesterday.

"I make one sorry knight, I'm afraid."

"And I make one sorry princess."

I smile back and do not know what to say for a moment. I feel like the fifteen-year-old again. Molly has that ability.

"Would you like something to drink?" I finally ask.

"No, thank you. I would like you to sit down, and we'll continue the story, if you don't mind."

I nod, sit down across from her, and take out my iPhone again.

"So, where were we?" she asks.

I start to say something but then stop myself. I feel my head being immersed in a steamer. A vision of middle-aged Molly, sun-browned and stark-naked, arrives unbidden but oh so cheerfully in my mind.

"Ah, yes, I remember now," the centenarian Molly says from her wheelchair. "I'm afraid my hopping-out-of-bed-in-my-birthday-suit days are long over."

I chuckle awkwardly and ask, "What happened afterward?" There are so many questions I want to ask, with an overriding one concerning John Pressman, but I don't. I will let the story unspool at its own pace. Molly is not one to be rushed, even at this stage in her life.

"What happened afterward?" she asks, and her eyes stare past me, heading east, across a half-dozen states and fifty-plus years into the past. "Bliss, my dear. Complete and total bliss."

CHAPTER 19

1961
MOLLY

Life has no purpose except what you give it. That's what Molly knew in her old age, and looking back on her life, she understood its defining moment was the first night John shared her bed and the immediate weeks following it.

Intellectually, she recognized the summer could've lasted only so many days, but, in remembrance, it seemed to last epochs, from the creation of the Milky Way to its expiration. Not because the time was dull but rather it was so damn *fun* and so life-affirming, it could've been a magical potion concocted to revive the dead.

Even in her advanced age, she could see that time, so clearly delineated in what the novelist John Dos Passos called the Camera Eye—mental snapshots, frozen in bliss, which neither age nor time could mar their perfection.

Except those images weren't exact captures of reality. No, the Camera Eye was also suffused with what photographers called the Golden Hour—the gilt-tinted hour following sunrise and preceding sunset, when the world was awash with russet rays and even the meanest streets were aglow as if in an Arthurian legend. Every moment spent with John was like that, reality beyond reality. Richer, realer, rawer than reality.

These were the moments she remembered most.

When John asked Molly if she wanted to go to work with him, she said yes, and the next thing she knew, they were bouncing along in his Rambler to various points of her city. Except these were on the proverbial "other side of the tracks," and she was reminded of when she'd taught *Walden* to her 11th-grade American Lit class. The more perceptive students had snickered when she'd read aloud Thoreau's boast, "I have traveled a good deal in Concord," and she had even smiled herself.

But now she knew you could indeed be well-traveled even if you hadn't gone far—and she had not traveled a good deal in her own hometown. No, she had not one bit, and she recalled another famous quote: "Whereas I was blind, now I see."

And see she did.

The humble but well-maintained shotgun shacks, their thin, multicolored clapboard walls like vibrant set pieces in a Hollywood film. The broken down, defeated roads—no city funding here—and what had defeated them: the rolling landscape of relentless tall grass and brush, the green appearing at first one-toned and overwhelming, but when Molly looked more closely, she spotted islands of yellow and white and blue wildflowers, like vibrant archipelagoes in a deep emerald sea. The tiny convenience stores, white-walled and lonely, that appeared here and there in the undulating Mississippi afternoons like way stations or desert oases, with the invariable trio of old men out front, their gossiping ceasing when John and Molly stepped out of the car but recommencing when they realized the two meant no harm and only wanted to buy Cokes. This world, this beautiful, magnificent, unknown world that had always been so achingly close to her own ... She had never experienced it but now wanted to, with abandon.

And experience she did. In churches, in school cafeterias, in restaurants over plates of ham hock and black-eyed peas. The mid-summer heat was pervasive, but it was equally uncomfortable when a hundred pairs of eyes stared at John and her whenever they entered a new meeting place. "Like two grains of salt dropped into a jar of pepper," was Bethanee's smirking verdict, and Molly, who'd been judged all her life because of her gender, felt for the first time what it was like to be judged by her color.

But then folks found out who they were. The white man who had stopped the bully at the diner and his lady, a local gal but one on their side, and the suspicion was dispelled. In those weeks, she remembered a blur of meetings and how John won over everyone. Here was a new role that she observed in him. Not as a chef but as an organizer, speaker, advocate, *leader*. All these manifold parts were from one person and that one person was comfortable in each part.

And each part loves me, Molly thought and felt a near-delirium of bliss.

Plans were hatched and described. Alliances were formed. Which section of town to stage further sit-ins, when was the right time to have a parade, how much steel did the mayor and the chief of police have in their backbones?

So this is what it feels like to be a part of history. I am standing near the epicenter of history. A bit off-center, true, but nonetheless close enough to feel its first rumblings. She was awed by this knowledge.

Late one night, after a strategy session with a local civil rights group, Molly and John and company were introduced to a juke joint along a tributary of the Mississippi River. From the outside, the place looked like a mechanic's shop with haphazard, corru-gated-metal walls. Inside, it was a hazy heaven of dancing bodies, singing voices, and drinking forms whose every gesture was of inebriated happiness.

Molly was happy too, drinking and—she hardly believed this afterwards—jitterbugging with John Pressman of New York … and knowing she was part of a group that helped tilt the world just a tiny bit the right way. Yes, she, one tiny person, was part of it. Hardly noticeable, true, but "hardly" was more than nothing. "Hardly" made all the difference in the world in how she saw herself.

She learned something else too, something that John had said:

Only by *not* fixating on your own happiness but on that of others could you truly be happy.

Molly had a hammock, a dusty thing she had purchased from a Sears Roebuck catalog a decade earlier. It lay neglected in an even dustier corner of her garage, like so many of her other projects fallen by the wayside of life. But John spied it one afternoon and brought it out, his eyes sparkling like a little boy's. They cleaned it and set it up between a fig tree and a post in her backyard.

Twice a week, they lay on the hammock and drank beer, watching the late-afternoon sunrays light up the world with their amber glow. She lay wrapped in his thick arms, her fingertips tracing the brass grill on his one-of-a-kind watch, and felt so singularly secure.

The modern woman in her wanted all the rights afforded modern women—or should afford women, modern or not—but another part of her liked being pampered and protected, like some Victorian woman. A Victorian woman minus the all-constricting corset, of course.

She smiled at that image and said, "I've never done this before. Just lie here and, I don't know, enjoy the moment."

John nodded and took another sip of his beer. "No?"

"No, not even with Aaron," Molly said and wondered why she'd brought up her ex-husband. Aaron—how familiar the name once was and how alien it had become.

"Especially not with him," she added, shaking her head, thinking of all those wasted years.

John said nothing and looked at her. She wasn't sure if he wanted elaboration, but she proceeded to give it anyway. Likely more for her own sake than his.

"On the outside, we were picture perfect," she said. "He was from a prominent local family of lawyers, and he himself became a lawyer. We had a large brick house overlooking the river, and our driveway could've come from a car catalog. You know, the waxed, late-model Caddy for the hubby and the sensible station wagon for the missus. On paper, at least, you could say we were US Steel. But in reality ..."

She stopped talking, and John drew her closer, so close she could hear his heart beat, slow and steady and strong, as it always was.

Molly wondered this: *Could the size of man's soul be small?* She marveled that she would ask herself this question, for the obvious answer was yes. After all, if John's was infinitely large, then his polar opposite must also surely exist. Her ex-husband's soul was very small indeed. He was forever spinning his wheels to enlarge his soul, to fill its emptiness, with *things*. The luxury car, the large house, the high-paying but unimaginative job, the respect of people he didn't even like. Like so many men, he needed a boy's toy box of *things* to feel whole. John was the opposite. He didn't need anything to feel whole besides a hammock, a beer, and *her*.

"What about you, John?" she asked him, glad to have finally, firmly put her ex-husband in the past. "Any special someone from your misspent youth?"

"A couple." He was smiling as he answered her. "But in terms of outrageous sex appeal, they're not even in the same zip code as you."

"Oh, I'm sure of that. But only a couple? Really now. I remember you telling me how you weren't in the war."

"Yeah, I was rejected for service because of a mastoid operation in my left ear."

"That's what I'm saying. The male-female ratio in New York during the war must've been heavily tilted in your favor. What do you say to that, Mister Only-A-Couple?"

John's smile had stretched to Cheshire Cat dimensions. "I'm not sure how reliable my memory is. But I do vaguely remember a couple—well, maybe more than a couple—waitresses who for some unfathomable reason decided to chase me. I have to admit, I allowed myself to be caught more than a couple of times."

He laughed hard when Molly, in a dramatized gesture of pique, poured the rest of her beer over his head.

She and John sat in his Rambler one morning, parked downtown. They were silent, and though she was hungry, she suspected even if John had cooked a French feast sumptuous enough to satisfy Louis XIV, she wouldn't have been able to take a single bite. Her sense of taste had deserted her as had her sense of smell, leaving only touch as an all-purpose outlet for her anxiety. She felt not only butterflies in her stomach but a whole farm of fluttering monarchs, swallowtails, and painted ladies.

Through the windshield, she could see the gray-bricked building that housed the downtown Woolworth's Department Store, and though it was a popular place, she never recalled a crowd waiting out front when it opened at 10 a.m. News reporters with their cameras and, with melancholy police separating them, another group, holding not cameras but placards. "Race-Mixing Is Communism" and "Communist Jews Behind Race-Mixing" were some of the delightful phrases, and something died inside Molly when she spied Sally Harper, Cash's mother and Police Chief Hollis's wife, among the group. But no gremlins in white sheets. Thank God for that.

Still surreal, though, Molly thought, seeing the scene in front of her, at a location she had walked by a thousand times before. She had always thought history was made up of grand gestures, as recent, momentous events seem to demonstrate. The British Prime Minister kowtowing to the Nazi Fuehrer at Munich, the quarter-million troops landing on D-Day, the two atomic bombs that ended World War II.

But now she knew better. History could be judged grand even if the event was, on the surface, small. For here, right in front of her, was history in the flesh, history that would be immortalized in print and film. The city council and mayor had surrendered, and evidently so had the biggest department store in town.

Here, beyond the windshield, was the truism of John's saying— the amazing was right below the surface of the everyday—once again confirmed. Now, they just had to wait, and Molly prayed that her town, the place she'd grown up in even if she had always felt apart, her extended family, would not disappoint her again.

Then she saw them—a young mother holding the hands of her two children, one boy of around ten, the girl seven. They were smartly dressed and walking with dignified steps toward the entrance of Woolworth's, a minute or so before the ten o'clock opening, as if the woman had timed it. There was nothing remarkable here except one superficially meaningful but actually meaningless thing: the three were black.

They stared straight ahead, ignoring everyone—the news reporters, the placard-brandishing protesters—and concentrated on the door, which was being opened by a young, white-uniformed man.

Inside the Rambler, Molly took John's hand. The mother and her two kids hesitated just an instant before the young white man, and then the man smiled, and he said—Molly couldn't hear him but nonetheless knew what was said—"Welcome to Woolworth's, ma'am." Then the family went inside, accompanied by the flash of cameras and the enraged shouts from the placard wavers.

"Well, there's that," John said and squeezed her hand. She looked back at him, but through her abrupt tears, she couldn't see him too clearly.

"You ever feel like you're going backwards in time?" Bethanee said.

It was a Sunday afternoon, quiet and hot, in the common room of the Jupiter Hammon College dormitory. Molly sat finishing up Michener's *Hawaii* and waiting for John to freshen up in the bathroom so they could go on their first bonafide date in weeks.

Bethanee was sitting across the room, also reading, and being the consummate bibliophile, Molly made sure to notice the title: *1984*.

She was relieved to also discover the space between her and the young woman no longer crackled with tension. Instead, a grudging silence had become the prevailing condition until Bethanee asked her question.

"How so?" Molly said and put down her book.

"What I mean is, you're what? Fifty, right? Yet here you are, picking up your gentleman caller at some college dorm like you're twenty again."

"I think I'm the gentleman caller in this case," Molly said and smiled. She could no longer feel insulted by this brave but often very silly girl. Besides, she didn't mind living a twenty-year-old's life—or a fifty- or even eighty-year-old's. Any age would do, as long as she got to spend it with John Pressman of New York.

But then she realized Bethanee wasn't trying to be offensive as the young woman asked, "Why don't you just ask him to live with you?"

Molly started to say something then stopped. She was stumped, and it took a moment for her to realize why. Like racial attitudes, gender mores were hard to overcome, particularly since she'd spent a lifetime unquestioningly living under the latter, if not the former. She was just thinking how to start this awkward explanation—how, if she and John lived together without being married, they would be living in sin—when someone entered the room from the outside, providing a thankful escape.

It was the young man whom Molly had gotten to know well these last couple of weeks. The shivering volunteer drenched with lemonade at The Porky Pie diner. William—he of the shy, adorable smile and shirts and pants so pressed and creaseless, they looked like cartoon clothes.

"Hello, Miss Valle."

"Hi, William, how are you?"

"Fine," he said, then turned his attention to Bethanee, who regarded him with a smile of genuine amusement, though what *kind* of amusement it held, Molly didn't want to dwell on.

William said to the young woman, "Remember ..."—and that was all, as if the effort to exhale that single word made everything else that should've followed impossible.

"Yeah, I know," Bethanee said, and William paused for a long moment then nodded and walked—no, *slunk*—away into the back.

Molly, who had seen her share of classroom crushes, thought, *Man, he has it bad.* The proverbial puppy if there ever was one.

"He wants me to listen to one of his songs," Bethanee explained to Molly. "And you know what? He ain't half-bad."

"Is that what he wants to become? A musician?"

"Sure, and if wishes were horses, beggars would ride. No, if he's not careful, he'll end up a dentist like his father wants him to be. But you know what's funny? He reminds me of someone you know."

"Me? Who's that?"

"That white boy having the hissy fit with you at the market."

"Cash?"

"That's the one. Well, he came by one of our meetings the other day."

Cash ... Molly had to shake her head in wonder. Her student. Her *former* student. The son of the town's police chief *and* of an enraged woman holding one of those ugly signs in front of Woolworth's. Cash Harper attending a civil rights meeting.

"I chewed the fat with him a bit," Bethanee continued. "It's funny. Up close, he's the spitting image of his cop daddy. But he's ... different. I'll give him that. He asked me how he could help."

Molly nodded. *Wonders never cease.*

"You know, he asked about you too. You're his old teacher, right?"

"Yes. What did you say?"

"The truth. That you were over the moon. But then even Helen Keller could see that."

Molly wasn't sure where this conversation was going and was expecting another putdown. But it never came as Bethanee eyed her a moment then heaved a sigh, which sounded strangely both resigned and admiring.

"You know, John's the fish you snagged hook, line, and sinker. At the time, I couldn't see how you did it, but now I know."

"What do you mean?"

"I should've seen that you're irresistible to men."

Molly laughed, surprised and incredulous. Attractive maybe, even a little pretty once—those descriptions she could buy. But irresistible? No, that word was reserved for screen sirens like Sophia Loren, Jayne Mansfield, and Marilyn Monroe. Definitely not Molly Valle of Small Town, Mississippi.

"I wish that were true, Bethanee. But based on the number of failed dates I've had, I'm afraid it's not."

But the young woman was already shaking her head at Molly, like a parent to a child for not understanding a basic arithmetic problem.

"I said irresistible to *men*," Bethanee said. "Those dates you were on, they were with *boys*. And speaking of boys, I'd better go see William before he dies of impatience." She rolled her eyes and fluttered her fingers at Molly. "Ta ta."

A minute after Bethanee had disappeared into the back, John emerged. Gorgeous, damp-haired John in his form-fitting denims. The Marlboro Man minus the nicotine-stained fingers and, admittedly, the thirty-inch waist.

"What's funny?" he asked her.

She didn't know she had been smiling. "Everything, love, everything."

Sunday morning in her kitchen. She had just made breakfast for him. Nothing hoity-toity like the French fare she imagined he served at Rockefeller Center but good old Americana: scrambled eggs, bacon, buttered toast. She was wrapped in her dowdy, tea-pot-themed bathrobe and poured real tea from a real teapot. She watched him eat, clad in his boxers and nothing else, the brawny arm with its purposeful movements with the fork to the plate to those kissable lips above the lickable chin scar.

Feeding my man, Molly thought and enjoyed the pleasure that phrase evoked.

"Hmmm?" he said, looking up.

"Just eat."

As John returned to his plate, she couldn't help but wonder, *But is he really my man?* She wasn't sure anymore. Some of the certainty that had come from that enchanting night, just a few weeks ago, had departed. He was her man now, but how long would that *now* last? His job was nearly done here, in her town.

As if to reinforce her doubt, he said, "I need to get to the college today. Help Bethanee and William pack up."

She nodded and said nothing. Better to not think about it. Better to return to what she'd done toward the end of summer for the past quarter-century: look over lesson plans for the upcoming school year. Not that she was even sure she'd have a job come September.

Still, thinking of school reminded her of something:

"If you see my old student, Cash, there, telephone me, okay? I'd like to see him."

John nodded. "You care about him, don't you?"

"I've known him almost since he was born. He's … well, almost …"

"Like a son?"

"I guess you can say that," she said and tried not to think of the steam-issuing-from-his-ears way Cash had spoken to her at the market.

John picked up his empty plate, stood up, and went to the sink. He began to wash the plate and fork, his back to her. He asked her, "Have you ever thought of having a child?"

The question, so gauche, so unlike John, stunned her. Rocked her like a corporeal blow. Not out of left field but out of the left field in a stadium from across the city.

"No, like I've said, we—Aaron and I—never worked it out. And me … well, it's too late now, isn't it? Why would you ask such a thing?"

John put the plate in the dish rack, came back, and sat down.

"You can always adopt one," he told her and took one of her abruptly hot hands in his. "No, I take that back. What I meant to say was, '*We* could adopt one.'"

"What?" she began, her anger dissipating in a flash. And before her mind could even register the action, John had, with his free hand, slid a ring across the tabletop.

"Will you marry me, Molly Valle?" John Pressman asked, on his knees, both of his hands on hers now. She didn't remember him getting into that position. Her shock had blanked her out for a couple of seconds, it seemed. He was speaking again, and she only caught the tail end: "… don't want to leave here without you. Don't want to leave any place without you."

Oh my. Molly put her hand to her no-doubt agape mouth. *Oh my, oh my, oh my.*

After her divorce, she hadn't thought this day would ever come again, but here it was, a second proposal. *Life is funny*, she thought, and she felt herself step back from the reality of her situation for a moment, lest its emotions overwhelm her and make her swoon like a damsel in those Middle English chivalric romances she taught in 10th-grade English.

Yes, life was indeed funny. It had no syllabus, which was why Molly, always a diligent student, felt so unprepared for it. Life played tricks on you too, surprised you, with the biggest surprise that life, even at the nearly half-century mark, could still hold surprises.

Like so: *There is a man in my kitchen, a man I'm in love with, and he wants to spend the rest of his life with me.* How strange and how very unconventional by its conventional, everyday setting. But love didn't have to take place in a chalet on the Swiss Alps, now did it? There could be a snow globe of a Swiss chalet, below which were two people madly in love and making love on a twin-sized mattress in a third-floor Bronx walkup. That image, absurd though it was, nonetheless contained the truth. And it held another truth:

People gave up too soon on their dreams. Molly didn't expect to live beyond the average age of seventy-something, which meant she had found her dream after two-thirds of her life had already passed. Yes, people gave up too soon on dreams and hope, but both were there, if you kept your eyes open.

With that truth in mind, she returned to the world only to find her own eyes were so tear-filled, she might as well have been submerged fifty feet underwater.

"Yes, I will marry you, John," she heard herself say. "Of course, I will. You kidding me?"

She laughed and wiped her eyes, no longer fifty feet underwater but skimming the surface of a great, churning sea. John reached up and kissed her, and they stayed like that for a minute, a month, a millennium.

Then she was putting on the ring. She didn't remember the kiss having ever stopped. It was as if she were watching a movie of her own life with abrupt, inexpert cuts. The ring was nicked here and there, as if it had been used to parry blows in a knife fight. It was also much too large. It hung on her ring finger like an inner tube around a child's beanpole torso. The ring was one of the most beautiful things she'd ever seen.

"It's bit big, I admit," John said. "It belonged to my grandmother, who held a scythe half her waking hours in the Ukraine, so her hands were a bit bigger than yours."

Molly held up her hand, admiring the much-too-big ring that slid down her finger. "It's wonderful. But how did you get it?"

"I called my sister in New York, and she mailed it to me."

She looked at him. "When was that?"

"I called the morning after our first date at the diner."

Molly laughed, and then she and John kissed again. In the middle of her humdrum kitchen that actually contained Aladdin's lamp and all the wishes it could grant.

There was no happily ever after in mortal life, she knew, but fairy tales did exist. They just didn't last forever, but she hoped, if she and John took good care of themselves, they'd be laughing another twenty, thirty, or even forty years. And that would be good enough for the fairy tale of her life.

What Molly didn't know, however, was that her fairy tale would end much sooner than she'd hoped, and the beginning of its ruin would occur with something as inconsequential as a phone call.

CHAPTER 20

MOLLY

The call came while Molly was putting into reality her and John's plan, namely packing to elope to New Orleans. There, they would marry and spend a weekend honeymooning before returning to her hometown on Monday and telling everyone, "Voila, we're married!"

Elope—the word conjured in her mind absurdly romantic notions of youth and excitement. She certainly felt thrilled attired in a new airy, summer dress with a sunflower pattern and stuffing the picnic basket with food, wine, and—she was a reader before anything else—her just-finished *Hawaii* for him and the new Irving Stone bestseller, *The Agony and the Ecstasy*, for herself.

Meanwhile, the *him* in question was strutting across the living room to the garage, a coil of rope in his hands. Molly stifled a giggle, thinking, What did he think they were going to do in the Big Easy, alpine-climb? But that peccadillo could be forgiven since

John, in his white T-shirt and black jeans, looked more *Wild One* than Brando did in the actual movie.

So, this is domestic bliss.

Molly laughed to herself, her cheeks slightly pained from all the smiling she'd been doing lately. She felt the overly large ring hanging in a string around her neck and thought again that she was in a movie.

No, that wasn't quite right. Not a movie but a painting, something Seurat or Signac would draw, something pointillist and wonderful. What was that famous painting called? *A Sunday Afternoon on the Island of La Grande Jatte.* Yes, that was it. Well, her painting would be called *A Friday Afternoon in the House of La Grande Dame*—though, it would be stretching the rubber band well past the snapping point to call herself "grande."

She was still chuckling at her own presumption when the telephone rang. She frowned. Nobody called her these days except the hate-filled folks, and she steeled herself before picking up the handset.

"Hello."

"Molly, it's Bethanee. I need to speak to John."

"Sure," Molly said, a new unease supplanting the original one. She called toward the garage, "John, it's Bethanee on the phone!"

When John returned and picked up the phone, she deliberately went outside to check out the two bikes trussed to her car rack. She felt the sunshine on her face and tried to let its comforting warmth assuage her rapidly beating heart. A simple phone call, she told herself. That's all there was to it. Yet she knew she was telling herself a lie. When she went back inside a few minutes later and saw John sitting on the living room couch, his glorious, sun-bronzed face fixed in an uncharacteristic frown, she knew she had been right.

"What is it?" she asked, but she already knew.

The real world was returning, like a familiar but unwelcome family member, to her fantasy world. No, not returning but *intruding*. The real world and its ever-present responsibilities, benign on the surface yet anything but underneath.

Responsibilities that dug into people's lives like termites and then *grew*, until only a minuscule part of each day was a person's own. Responsibilities that, as surely as a catastrophic event but one stretched out across years and even decades, destroyed most people's dreams. The lesson-planning and paper-grading that decimated the teacher's novelist dreams (she herself had had them once). The children's orthodontic costs that sabotaged the housewife's career-training classes. The enervating office jobs that countless people had to work to ensure their family's health and well-being but shattered their own ...

Such was life, Molly knew, and, in general, she didn't particularly mind it. Didn't she not too long ago even welcome all those responsibilities that would inevitably come with being John Pressman's wife? Yet, didn't she and John deserve at least *one* weekend?

"Bethanee wants us to go to Atlanta," John told her and explained why. The young woman had already embarked on their organization's next step—riding in integrated buses to challenge the South's Jim Crow public transportation laws, stopping in segregated bus depots from Virginia to New Orleans. The first bus had left its

Washington, DC starting point several days ago and would soon be in Georgia. The volunteers had been sitting in pairs—black, white, black, white—but one of the white couples had been frightened by the violence in Rock Hill, South Carolina and decided to quit the rest of the ride.

"That's where we step in," John said. "We're the replacements. Bethanee is leaving tonight, and she said the drive would take nine hours to Atlanta."

Molly sighed, sat down, found herself saying, "Can't she find someone else?"

He sat down beside her. "She wouldn't ask if she had someone else."

"I guess we've got to go then," she said, knowing she didn't want to but knowing the alternative was impossible. Even if—and she didn't know why, but she felt it—the action could be life-threatening. She knew how the people of her town behaved, but she wasn't sure about the other cities in Mississippi or in the surrounding states. Based on the scenes when Little Rock Central High integrated a few years ago, she wasn't hopeful.

"Is that what you want, Molly?"

She looked up and shook her head. "No, but what can we do, right?" She knew how John felt about Bethanee, as a daughter who, headstrong and incautious, needed protection.

So, here was an impasse, the fabled fork in the road. Molly, knowing this fact, said nothing more. John likewise seemed to understand and also said nothing.

The sun had dipped low enough in the afternoon sky so its rays slanted into her living room like orange-gelled spotlights on a Broadway stage. The air was warm and for once not too hot. Quiet except for the birdsong right outside her window. It was a perfect late-summer Mississippi day in 1961, one indeed worthy of a painting.

But not one by Seurat. Nothing so meticulous and planned. She had been wrong about that. No, her painting—*their* painting, her and John's—was inchoate, not even at the halfway point, just a few random brushstrokes on a white, gessoed canvas. But she also knew something else. It would only need a few more seconds of work to complete their painting, and how it would turn out depended entirely on what they would do next.

Then the painting was indeed finished as John said, "There's another possibility, where we can have our cake and eat it too. We could get their bus route, have our weekend together, then meet up with them in whatever place they'll be on Tuesday. We'll get married and can still have our honeymoon just like we planned. What do you think about that?"

She tried to keep her smile from appearing but gave up after a second.

"I think that's an idea worthy of the Nobel Prize Committee," she said and laughed.

Those enervating responsibilities could indeed coexist with their love and dreams. They could indeed have their cake and eat it too. All twelve sugary, frosting-stuffed layers of it.

John said, "I'll call Bethanee," and picked up the phone.

And so ended their last chance at happiness.

CHAPTER 21

MOLLY

Bethanee died.

She had gotten on the bus as she'd wanted in Atlanta. The group had been surprisingly welcomed in Georgia's capital, had indeed met with Martin Luther King, who'd stopped by for dinner in a popular black-owned restaurant to offer them his encouragement. Full of good cheer and resolve, the group had set off the next morning for Alabama.

There, it happened.

After leaving a depot in Anniston, the driver discovered two of his tires had been slashed, and when he pulled over right outside the city, a mob descended on the Greyhound. Filled with rage and seeming superhuman strength, the mob rocked the bus back and forth, as if the very demon of intolerance was shoving the vehicle.

Inside, the group tried to stay calm and collected and waited for the authorities to arrive. They never did. Without warning, there were two firebombs—twin explosions followed by the hiss of spreading, sizzling liquid on the roof. Black smoke appeared, and it was the smoke, more than the fire and the mob, that the passengers feared most of all.

"We must leave *now*," the passengers remembered Bethanee shouting. She was not the leader of the group, this slight young woman with the oddly retro clothes, but at that moment, like in all times of crisis, titles on paper meant nothing. She *was* their leader, and as smoke proceeded to choke the Greyhound's interior, she popped the front door open. To show there was nothing to be afraid of, she was the first to exit and therefore the first to meet the rabid mob.

People said that the moment seemed to freeze in time, Bethanee in heroic mid-step, as calm as a Christian martyr before the lions. But she never got beyond that self-propelled movement because a bullet, fired from a line of trees some hundred yards away, felled her before she'd even set her foot on the gravel. She was killed in an instant, and her death made the front page in every single newspaper in the country.

It was in one of those newspapers where Molly and John discovered their colleague's death. The new husband and wife—they had married just that morning—had finished a late lunch in the French Quarter of New Orleans when they walked in front of a newspaper kiosk.

Hand in hand, they were both filled with the ecstasy of dreams, except Molly didn't remember ever having one that possessed such sustained euphoria. She was still musing over this strange miracle—how her reality had become more fantastic than the most hallucinatory unreality—when she, for no reason at all, glanced at the paper stand and saw the front page of *The Times-Picayune* and the photo of the ablaze Greyhound.

She remembered giving a short, truncated cry, and then she felt her hand pressed against her mouth, as if she were afraid her life could be exhaled from between her lips. Frozen, she watched as John strode past her, picked up the paper, read the first paragraph, and then he, easily the strongest man she had ever known, sank to one knee, fighting collapse. The collapse, Molly knew later, not only of his body but of every chance of happiness he and she would have in life.

The funeral was large, and people from all over the country came to it. Molly, sitting beside John in the front pew, went through it in a daze, seeing the world as if through a window blasted by torrential rain.

"I should've been there," John whispered when the funeral was over but they were still sitting. Molly shook her head but didn't know what to say.

She was still silent when they stepped out onto the parking lot and witnessed William sagging against his car. John strode over and bear-hugged William, as if by holding the weeping young man as tightly as he could, he could somehow prevent him from falling apart. Could maybe even prevent himself from crumpling too.

The police never found out who Bethanee's killer was, the coward in the woods with the rifle. Or so they said. The world would never know.

Life went on, and Molly tried to return to some semblance of a normal one with her new husband. But there really was no normal in sharing a life with John Pressman. For several years, theirs was a peripatetic one of motel rooms, guest rooms in civil rights organizers' homes, and dorms at black colleges throughout the South.

Here was the life of adventure she'd always sought but never believed she would achieve. More importantly, it was coupled with a purpose that made human life worthwhile. The promotion of voting rights, school rights, desegregation across an entire landscape of the earth. Yes, those were the best years of her life, as she left her forties and passed the half-century mark.

She didn't know why, but she would sometimes glimpse Bethanee out of the corner of her eye. The young lady slipping an envelope into the mailbox down the block, the woman pushing the shopping cart at the end of the aisle, the one in a station wagon full of screaming kids … They were all Bethanee's doppelgängers until Molly, seeing them up close, realized the women didn't look the least bit like her.

At those moments, she would think, *That woman is too old to be Bethanee*, because Bethanee, had she lived, would only be twenty-two. Thinking of that number, which inevitably grew as Molly herself aged, she would wonder what Bethanee would be doing, and that thought, like a destructive chemical over photo negatives, would render monochrome all the colors of her day.

One night in 1964, in a flop hotel in Memphis, they watched President Johnson on TV announce the passage of the Civil Rights Act. Afterward, John turned to her and said, "If only Bethanee could've seen this."

Molly thought, *Don't*, but couldn't help but nod.

He returned the nod, smiled briefly, then nodded again, as if encouraging the smile to make a second appearance. It never did. They sat in silence in their room, which reeked of the previous occupant's stale cigarettes. They watched the gray cube of talking heads but no longer heard a word.

Then, with his eyes still fixed on the TV, John asked her, "That Friday when we decided not to go with her—why do you think we did that?"

"Why?" Molly asked, as if twirling the question about, uncertain. But she needn't pretend for she long had a ready-made answer. Yet why did she still feel so sickly hot all of a sudden?

"We thought she would be safe," she told him. "We thought we would meet her later on, remember? On Tuesday."

"Was that really it? Or did we not go because we were afraid? That something like *that* was going to happen?"

"John ... don't do this." She heard herself say the words, echoey and strangely disembodied, and she didn't even know what they meant, specifically the word "this." What was "this"? John's questioning of her statement? His dredging up the past? Or his shining a flashlight beam finally through the flimsy veil of their self-serving lies?

"We did that, didn't we, Molly? At the moment when we could've either accepted our responsibilities or neglected them, we chose the latter."

"It wasn't neglecting our responsibilities. It was living our dream."

"Yeah, there's that," John said, but his words were as brittle as desiccated leaves. He stood up and went into the bathroom and closed the door behind him.

Molly wanted to spring up, stride to the door after him, and slam her hand repeatedly against it. She wanted to scream how unfair it was for him to blame themselves for what had happened, as if their only choice were to choose between their dream—their wedding, their whole life together—and getting on the bus a couple of days earlier, as if life's decisions were strictly made up of binary parts, either 1 or 0 and no other number. And even if they had been on the bus, what goddamn difference would it have made?

But she didn't get up. She stayed sitting in the room whose shadows seemed to have deepened since John left. She was fifty-one years old, and she knew some things in life could not be explained by logic. Some things could not be deciphered by intelligence, some puzzles whose solution went beyond reason and brainpower.

The unsolvable puzzle was this: how did you find joy again in life when you knew that a young woman had died because, at a finite moment of weakness, she and John had neglected their responsibilities? All those beautiful lessons she had learned from John couldn't overcome this truth and its crushing guilt. They just lessened them like aspirin would a migraine, partially dulled but the core pain ever-present underneath.

Bethanee would be twenty-five now.

The period that historians later would call the civil rights era slowly drew down, and the right side ended in glorious triumph. However, having burned her bridges in her hometown, Molly could no longer stay there or even in the South in general. Too much bad blood and too many bad memories.

In 1968, she and John moved to southern California to be with her only remaining relative, her aspiring actor brother, who never became the next Anthony Quinn but did make a respectful living installing air-conditioning units in the tract homes rapidly spreading across Orange County. They pooled their life savings and squeezed out a down payment on a small condominium there, and Molly found a teaching job at a local high school and John a head chef position at a mid-tier Italian restaurant.

They never adopted a kid like they once talked about doing, geological epochs ago in 1961.

But they still had each other, and they watched America grow old as they themselves did. Saw the world change as surely as their own reflections. Plane travel was no longer a luxury, and neither were long-distance phone calls. TV screens turned multicolored and so did magazines, black and white relegated to a forgotten, benighted past. Movies began having nudity and swear words, both of which were unbelievable to Molly.

To ground themselves in this rapidly changing world, she and John continued their volunteering, at soup kitchens and churches, wherever there was need. But their help was no longer centered on the monumental issues of the day. Like aging actors, they were shuffled to the side, into supporting roles, which was just as well. They had had enough excitement in their early middle years to last a lifetime.

Bethanee would be thirty-three now, fifty-nine-year-old Molly thought one day in 1971, out of the blue as always. She could picture the young woman, still bone-thin and regal-faced, attired in a flapper dress or some Edwardian-era cycling outfit. Nothing conventional, that was for sure. She might've been married or, more likely, still be single and a royal pain in the hindquarters. But alive.

Alive.

Thinking these sorrowful thoughts, Molly again wondered why she—and John, whom she found crying alone at times in their bathroom—punished herself after all these years.

They took trips, to New York to visit John's sisters and to Missouri to visit Cash Harper, the only person from her hometown with whom Molly had stayed in contact. The boy had not only grown to look nearly identical to his father but also had a near-identical job. He had become a small-town sheriff, his engineering wishes lost in the flotsam and jetsam of life like so many other people's dreams.

She herself had no major complaints about her own life. She and John had just finished making love in a motel in Key West when human beings first landed on the moon. They were at John's sister's Brooklyn apartment when a former B-movie actor became the most powerful man in the world. On the couch, Molly and John held each other's hands, both of which were ridged with blue veins.

Bethanee would be forty-two now. Fast approaching the age Molly had been when she'd met the love of her life … and then watched that shared love become eaten alive by shared guilt and grief.

But no love story, whether happy or otherwise, lasted forever, and even the best love stories ended by and large in the same spot—a hospital bed, an IV bag, lifeless fluorescent lighting, disinfectant smells. Molly found herself there one autumn night in 1987, sitting on a metal chair, John lying on the bed beside her, the once mighty body, the destroyer of bullies, long-shrunken by disease.

Destiny never existed, she now knew, and even if it did, what was its point when it would only bring her to this location?

Her husband of twenty-six years opened his eyes, noticed her beside him, and said softly, "You know, Molly, I just remembered that I've never told you something."

"Yes, John, what is it?" she said, standing up, feeling the movement in her bones.

"I don't think I've ever told you how beautiful you are."

She smiled despite herself. She knew she was no longer beautiful, not with her face crisscrossed with lines and her forty-eight-year-old body a quarter century and one hip replacement in the past. But John still believed it, and that was enough.

She said, "You've been telling me I'm beautiful every single day for the past twenty-five years."

"Have I?" His eyes arched up in mock surprise. "You'd better call the doctor then. I think she misdiagnosed me. Seems I'm actually suffering from Alzheimer's."

He started chuckling, and Molly did too. But soon the room dissolved in shimmering light as she began crying. Crying because John would soon leave her and she would be alone again. Crying that a man like John, so strong and brave, could be felled by something so lowly and ugly as prostate cancer—or that the life of a vibrant, headstrong, aggravating, beautiful young woman could be ended with something so sickeningly small as a fast-moving piece of lead.

"We had a good time together, didn't we, Molly?" her dying husband asked.

She was about to say, "A perfect time," when something stopped her, and as she continued crying, she couldn't pinpoint what exactly that was …

CHAPTER 22

THE PRESENT
RC

"Wait, that wasn't what happened."

The words are out of my mouth before I am even aware of them. A split-second later, I think of their cold-bloodedness in this moment, the heartbreaking end of Molly's story. Although I am sitting in her sun-drenched living room, I can still see the dark, antiseptic hospital room where the love of her life died three decades ago. But an image, no matter how powerful and melancholy, cannot overcome the reality of my memories.

You see, I was there thirty years ago, in the mid-1980s, not in the hospital, of course, but in this very living room. In fact, I was here *before* that terrible moment in the hospital, and John Pressman was not here then nor, more importantly, was his presence. There is something else too, something so blindingly obvious, that I missed it at first.

"No?" Molly asks, looking at me from her wheelchair, where she had been narrating for the past two hours. "Why do you say that?"

"Because you *were* on that bus," I say. "You're in the photo." Although I don't need to add the following, I think it: *the photo of you at forty-eight, screaming in front of the firebombed bus, the photo that brought me here.*

She says nothing to my assertion, but then again, what *can* she say? She closes her eyes and is silent for a while. I sit and wait. Through the half-opened blinds, the late-afternoon sunlight backlights her white hair so a corona has formed. Molly Valle looks like an angel—but an aged, fragile one. For a few moments, I wonder if her mind has been playing tricks on her, but no, that isn't the case. At more than twice my age, she still possesses a mind far sharper than I do. No, this frail angel lied to me.

Why?

Finally, she opens her eyes. "No, that wasn't what happened. But it was close, except for one difference." She raises her hand to stop any of my questions. "Come back tomorrow, RC, and I'll tell you what really happened. That story requires a bit more energy than I have right now. You understand, don't you?"

"Yes," I say and nod. Except I really don't. I don't want to wait till tomorrow. I want to know *now* what happened to her and John and Bethanee. What *actually* happened—the truth. But a voice deep inside tells me that I already know it, and it is this voice I want to silence, if by no other means than by confirming its own sad conclusions.

"Can I ask you just one question?" I say, and Molly gives a reluctant nod. "Did you really feel something terrible could've happened?"

"Yes, that part is true. When we received the call, I felt it, and I suspect John did too."

"But you did it anyway," I say, knowing what I long suspected was true. Neither she nor John went on their weekend getaway. They drove with Bethanee to the waiting Greyhound bus in Atlanta. "But why?" I ask.

"Because to not do something just because you're afraid of it—you can't live life like that."

I'm about to say, *Yes, but you could've done something else*, when I stop myself. Hindsight is always 20/20, and if Molly had known the bus would be firebombed, she could've called the state police or the Feds. But this would've been Monday morning quarterbacking of the worst sort. Hindsight would've allowed Molly to inform the police just like it would've helped a telegenic president bypass the front of a Dallas book depository. Unfortunately, reality is a tape player with no rewind button.

Yet ... yet, in a manner difficult to describe, I see it as more than this comforting picture. I know it, and I suspect Molly and John knew it at the time too. Both *did* know what could happen—I'm sure of it. And I am sure of something else: I am suddenly angry. What feels like a fiery bird spreads its wings inside my torso. But what or whom am I supposed to be angry at? Molly and John for their heroic, senseless, stupid decision? Or the world for being so cruel?

"You went there even though you knew it could mean the end of your dreams."

"Sometimes the most important thing you can do in life is to give up your dreams," Molly says and smiles a sad smile. "If you don't ...

well, why do you think I told you that story, RC? If we had evaded our responsibilities, the dream would've died anyway or, at the very least, turned into something neither John nor I could live with."

Reluctantly, I nod. I'm not sure if her story from the phone call onward is just a rationalization of her real decision—which, again, I still don't know—but it didn't feel like one. Her hypothetical future with John sounded right, from what I know about their selflessness and unshakeable sense of responsibility.

I abruptly recognize something else, and with this realization, my anger dissipates. They had no choice—none at all. I see this so clearly now, and I'm ashamed that I didn't earlier. Robert Frost wrote about "two roads diverg[ing] in a wood" and taking "the one less traveled." But, in Molly's case, both roads continued on to equally devastating destinations, even if the specifics were different. Which of the two paths would you choose if one went off a cliff and the other into quicksand?

Except she, who lost the most, obviously doesn't see her decision this way, and for the life of me, I can't see why. I don't know whether my failing is because I lack Molly and John's ability to see the reality behind the everyday or just a general stupidity on my part or, to put a pretentious spin on everything, some tragic flaw like out of classical Greek theater. I am missing something important here but am powerless to see what.

"Put a blanket on me," Molly says, "and please give me my remote. I'd like to watch the news a bit."

I shut off my voice recorder, fetch a blanket, and drape it over Molly's skeletal shoulders. She described John as the bravest person she had ever known, but knowing her current condition and the strength she conjures up every day to tell her story, I think the bravest person is actually the one she looks at each morning in the bathroom mirror.

"Should I stay, Molly? I can, you know. I'm on summer break for another month."

"No, the nurse will be coming in an hour for a final check," she says, and I nod. Then, without warning, she grips my wrist with surprising strength. She looks up at me, her brown eyes, despite being set in a landscape of wrinkles, appearing ageless and penetrating. Like they undoubtedly did a half-century earlier, when she confronted the bully in the diner.

"Don't feel sorry for me," she tells me. "That's the last thing I need."

"Okay," I say, chastened, and her grip falls away.

"Thank you for doing this," she says and smiles, the amiable and delicate old lady once again. "See you tomorrow, RC."

I keep my car radio on some hip-hop station as I drive home, hoping the loud music will distract me from my own troubling thoughts. Iggy Azalea, Nicki Minaj, Ariana Grande? I have no idea. It is the chirpy, synth-heavy music of the Millennials. Music that my Generation X ears can't quite appreciate, the same way I'd imagine Molly's WWII generation couldn't grasp my era's Hootie and the Blowfish, Pearl Jam, and the Smashing Pumpkins. Hootie and the Blowfish—to my high school students these days, that band might as well be Bach or Schubert. The world is passing me by too, little by little.

The music doesn't work as a distraction. Instead, it merely provides a discordant soundtrack to my own chaotic, seesawing thoughts, which I try to right like tiny boats in a Category 5 storm.

I have done no secondary research since I started listening to Molly's story, figuring why go to those sources—articles, books, the internet—when I have a primary source of the first order in *her*? Of course, I intend to, but only once her story is finished, which has been unfolding with all the spark and tension of a great novel. Now, the story is at the end, and I don't want to jump ahead. Except my mind tells me I already know the ending, even if my heart desperately craves another outcome.

Don't, my mind cautions, *don't do anything until tomorrow. Listen to what Molly has to say. Wait.* These thoughts are swirling as I grip the steering wheel far too tightly, my car going far too fast on the 405 Freeway, the sunrays like blowtorches in my eyes. I blink hard and reach for my iPhone, and I don't know whether I'm relieved or infuriated to find its battery dead.

Good, there's no way to check now. It'll take an hour to get home, and by then, this need—this crazy, obsessive need—will pass. Then you can wait till tomorrow.

I almost make it too except I spy those Golden Arches off an exit just as I leave Orange County and enter Los Angeles. Those Golden Arches that promise burgers, fries—and free WiFi.

As if watching a movie I can't control, I see my car cross three lanes of traffic, hearing belligerent honks but not caring in the least bit. See my car barely slow then screech to a stop in the McDonald's parking lot. With no apparent intermediate steps, I find myself standing and pulling out my laptop from my car trunk. I boot it up, and while Windows does its slow dance, I take my open laptop to my front passenger seat. Before I know it, I am Googling "John Pressman" and "civil rights."

My heart is pounding, hoping against hope that what I suspect isn't true. Or, at least, that the truth is some variation of Molly's lie. That she and John lived happily ever after—or as close to that myth as possible for mortals. That he passed away peacefully at a ripe old age in southern California.

But then the emerging Google Images grind to powder all my hopes, and I close my eyes. But it is no use. You see, I long ago saw the images. Every single one shows the photo. Molly screaming by the flaming bus. The photo that started everything.

I click on one of the images, and it fills my laptop's monitor. This time, however, I force myself away from Molly's face, whose anguish has doubtless always drawn the viewers' attention, including mine. Instead, I focus on the unconscious man lying face down beside her and notice, for the first time, the puddle of dark liquid formed beneath him.

"No," I say to myself, the word not of defiance but of resignation, as the grim pieces fall into place. I close my eyes so they can no longer be fooled by the photo's blurred, black-and-white nature. I open my *mind* and see the landscape in hideous color and 4K digital clarity. The man is blond and middle-aged; I can see the gray hairs mixed with the yellow. He has a husky build and, on one thick wrist, a strange, grill-faced watch.

And I know the man is not unconscious even before I read the caption below the photo: "Molly Valle, a civil rights worker, kneels beside the body of John Pressman, a fellow volunteer struck down by an unknown assassin's bullet and later confirmed dead at Anniston Memorial Hospital."

My laptop slides down my lap into the footwell. My mind pulsates with sadness, rage, and helplessness. I remember again Molly and John's advice to always look beneath the mundane for the hidden truth. Here, in this most mundane of locations—a McDonald's parking lot—I've found it. A sick version of it.

All love stories end unhappily, Molly told me, and I know hers did not end in a tranquil hospital room in 1987 but along a murderous stretch of road in Alabama in 1961, just a couple of months after she met John Pressman for the first time.

I also understand what she meant when she said everything in her story was true except for one difference. She had indeed been in a ragtag Memphis hotel in 1964, watching President Johnson's Civil Rights Act address. She had indeed been vacationing in Key West when Neil Armstrong stepped on the moon. Her visit to her former student Cash Harper in Missouri, her move to southern California, everything was the truth except for one thing.

She had been alone in every single one of these moments, John having died years then decades then a half-century earlier. A half-century without the love of her life—this realization hitting me like a slap from another, darker world. Molly Valle, the most beautiful and intelligent and selfless person I've ever known, has been alone all this time.

Rendered alone, after a lifetime of altruism—no, rendered alone *because* of one supreme act of altruism—by a monumentally unfair and vicious fate.

CHAPTER 23

THE PRESENT
MOLLY

After the young man left, Molly sits in her wheelchair and watches the evening news. She would prefer to read, but her eyesight makes this activity impossible, especially since she likes to read newsprint and not some tablet screen. She is, as she heard youngsters put it these days, *old school* like that.

And she never feels more old school than when watching the news. Walter Cronkite, "the most trusted man in America," is long dead, as are David Brinkley and Edward R. Murrow, her generation's powerhouses of investigative journalism. In contrast, the anchormen these days look to her either like male models or clowns minus the makeup.

The world of the 21st century is prettier and more convenient than in her day and, because of those qualities, maybe also duller.

People are no longer constantly afraid of nuclear annihilation, and the ghastly Jim Crow days are long gone. Indeed, America has already elected a black president, which was something Molly definitely did not expect to see in her lifetime. But then she did not expect her lifespan to reach triple digits either, a number which she has a hard time wrapping her head around, until her body's myriad aches make that easy to do.

Those pains reawaken as she turns off the TV and directs her electric wheelchair toward her kitchen. She has a nurse who comes by every night to check up on her, but damned if Molly has to share her home with a stranger during daylight hours. She can still move around, for God's sakes, albeit courtesy of battery-powered wheels that sound like inebriated canaries singing. She tries to see the humor in her plight and often can't, but then neither does she ever feel sorry for herself. Self-pity, in a world of famine and war, is an obscene self-indulgence.

But pity she did see in the eyes of RC, her writer-for-hire and, for the past several weeks, her rediscovered friend. Of course, RC is not his real name, which is so generic-sounding, it would fill pages in phone books from here to Des Moines. Besides, "RC" suits him.

The earnest and eager fifteen-year-old boy has grown up to be an earnest but very confused forty-four-year-old man. On his still unlined face—what is forty-four but a baby?—she perceived pity, which was the last thing she should've seen. It meant he didn't understand her story.

In her kitchen, she wheels over to her fridge and removes the pot with last night's chicken soup. She ignores the microwave, turns on a burner, and puts the pot on. *Old school indeed.* While her soup heats up, Molly thinks of RC again and of how wrong he is.

Her dream with John Pressman did die in Alabama over a half-century ago, but the dream he bestowed on her still lives. Tomorrow, she must make RC grasp this fact. Because, like many people, he only perceives one cruelty while being oblivious to another, more submerged and far-reaching one. Which is simply this: to see the world only as it often appears—callous and restricted, a landscape of unremitting grays and airless atmosphere, where once-rich, childhood dreams expire from asphyxiation. That love and adventure belong not to the real world but exclusively to the imaginary ones existing in pages, on celluloid, in the grooves of vinyl records, or to whatever the even more unromantic equivalents are in this increasingly cold, technological age.

Her time with John, brief though it was, showed her that love and adventure are very much real. They are not only the fantasies conjured up by writers, musicians, and filmmakers. They exist in the real world. *Magic exists*—a two-word phrase that, before her forty-eight-year-old self met John, she would've considered the ultimate in naiveté and self-delusion.

But it became very clear that it was her pre-John-Pressman self, her so-called realistic self, who had been naïve and self-deluded. She had known nothing, and then she had known paradise. She experienced paradise in this fallen world, and what was more, she experienced it in a location so reality-based—her hometown, her small house—that even now she is amazed it actually happened. But it did. *It did.* And if such beauty can exist in this fallen, benighted world, if even for just a few brief moments, then surely it is worthy to be saved.

This has been her life for the past fifty years, this striving to help save the world a little bit, to push it just a bit farther into the right. This action was the only thing that sustained her during the hard times, the hardest being the immediate years after John died and she'd come home after a long, wearisome day and find her rooms empty once again, his comforting smile and loving hands nothing but an ever-more-distant memory. In those times, only her purposeful life propped her up from total collapse, and she thought how strange that she had taught the morality play *Everyman* all those years but didn't fully understand its central lesson or how true it was until after she'd lost John:

We are our good deeds, and they alone will come with us into the afterlife.

In her southern Californian apartment, in the second decade of the 21st century, Molly thinks of that lesson again and draws comfort from the fact that she has lived a worthwhile life. And from something else too: she can still *see*. Indeed, even more adroitly than when John first taught her.

As her soup heats up, she wheels herself over to the window and looks out. Her home, situated atop a knoll, once had a vista of yellow grass all the way to the base of the low, green Santa Ana Mountains. No more. So-called progress has painted over that scene with Van-Gogh-thick brushstrokes. Now, there is nothing but the black lines of asphalt streets, the oversized shoeboxes of big-box stores—Target, Home Depot, Costco—and the cars moving like a never-ending stream of multicolored Lego pieces. Yet the late-afternoon sunshine that coats this most humdrum of views is the same warm, russet light that showcased all the past stories, magnificent or small, of this land. As Molly closes her eyes, she can see them all.

Sees the original people of this place, the Luiseño, fleet of foot and eagle-eyed as they hunted the rabbits and the antelopes that roamed the verdant mountains. Sees and hears the ringing bells for the first time at the Spanish mission of San Juan Capistrano—and the undiscovered and forbidden love affair between the conflicted Spanish priest and the obsidian-eyed Indian basket weaver. Sees, many centuries later, love affairs of a different, far shallower sort—those of the silent-screen stars as they made their weekend escapes from Hollywoodland to the primordial wilderness that was then Orange County. Sees, a couple of decades later, the Depression-era Okies, rag-dressed and hungry, trying to carve out a dignified life in the area's makeshift Hoovervilles.

These and a million other stories that Molly, with her eyes still closed, can see and explore. Stories all buried beneath the everyday, the Sam's Clubs, the Kentucky Fried Chickens, the Best Buys ... but no less unreal because of that interment. Magic exists.

"Thank you, John," Molly says, then opens her eyes.

The clouds are pastel coral reefs in the sunset sky, and the air is rich with summer sweetness. The nearby shopping center is aglow with neon store signs and LED headlights from curvy cars. Yes, the world has moved on from her era. Just about everyone from her generation is gone, and she knows she will soon join those departed. She wonders again if she will see John in heaven or if there is even such a place.

But she needn't wait for she can see him now. More than a half-century has passed, but he is standing next to her. She is standing too, and why not? She is only forty-eight, just beginning middle age, and with a middle-aged woman's strong legs and straight back. John is walking with her toward the Greyhound that will take them through the South in integrated defiance. He is nonchalantly chewing on half a Hershey's bar, the other half he's given to her. He is the most handsome he has ever been, with all the virility and character marks of the middle years. Just like Molly knows she's the most beautiful at this moment too. Forty-eight years old. Not too young, not too old, just right.

He must be afraid, she guesses. But his suntanned face doesn't show it. He walks with the insouciance of someone going to the grocery store. Of course, he *must* be afraid, just like she is, but he's long known how to suppress his own fear. He's driven it into a corner until it squeaked.

Dimly, dimly, in the back of her mind, Molly can smell warmed-up soup, delicious aromas, but not as delicious as the action of walking beside her lover.

She can see him clearly as he helps her up the first steps of the bus. Not that he needs to, but he has always been a gentleman. *My* gentleman, she thinks and laughs. She can smell his deodorant, Old Spice or maybe something else, something strong and elemental, something that fits him so very well. A step above him, she suddenly turns, bends down, and kisses him full on the lips, propriety be damned.

"I love you, John," she says when the kiss ends.

He smiles back and says, "We're on a great adventure."

And we are ...

Molly feels an ice cube travel up her spine. Except this sensation isn't followed by its usual giddiness but something else, something new. She has barely registered it as being different when she finds herself not sitting in her wheelchair but collapsed on the hardwood of her kitchen floor. Her first thought, spliced not with fear or pain, is of RC and how he will never hear the end of her story. The second is of John. Always of John.

She lies there on the kitchen floor, and she is still lying there when all the liquid in the soup has evaporated and the nurse lets herself into Molly's apartment an hour later.

CHAPTER 24

RC

Molly Valle is dead.

The thought numbs me as I sit toward the back of the nondescript chapel, located inside a nondescript mortuary by the 405 freeway. I saw the name of the place earlier, but I've blanked it out just like I want to blank out this whole scene, this whole reality.

The room is packed with people who knew Molly. One by one, they go up to the podium and eulogize her. They tell the assembled people what great a person she was and glance at the two photos of her on a nearby table festooned with flowers. One portrait is of her recent self, maybe in her nineties, I think, and the other—I wonder how they found this—is of her in her late forties, smiling by what I think is the Mississippi River. I think I know who took that photo, and the thought leaves me inside a deep, inky well.

Thankfully, there is no coffin or cremation urn, because either would be too much for me. So I concentrate on the current speaker, a woman who looks to be in her eighties. I see her lips move, and my ears register their sounds, but I hear nothing. A single thought, like an unstoppable tumor, has pushed aside all other functions in my mind:

Molly Valle is dead.

The sadness is still there, of course, but I've finished my crying. What remain are the numbness and the incomprehension. Eight days ago, she was alive and promised to tell me the end of her story. Seven days ago, I went to her apartment to find it locked, and a neighbor informed me that she had been taken to the hospital. There, I discovered she had passed away, and since then, I've been set adrift.

But then this unexpected event: five days earlier, I received a card in the mail asking for my attendance at Molly's funeral service. How they knew my address, I have no idea. Who "they" are is another unanswered question. I thought at first it must've been one of Molly's relatives, but then I remembered that her brother, the air-conditioner installer, passed away before she did. Could it have been one of his children, if he indeed had children?

I didn't know, and I still don't know. None of the speakers refer to Molly as a relative. No "Cousin Molly," no "Aunt Molly," no "Great-Aunt Molly."

"I first met Molly when we marched on Washington," a new speaker eulogizes. This is an elderly African-American man who relates their day at the March on Washington, when they heard Martin Luther King give his "I Have a Dream" speech. That was in August 1963, which was two years after the last event in Molly's story to me.

Something strikes me about this old man's speech. Actually, about all of the eulogies. No one here knew Molly like I knew her. That is to say, nobody knew her as far back as 1961, when she met John Pressman, when Molly Valle, by her own admission, became the Molly Valle being described at this moment. The man who commanded so spellbinding and luminescent a presence in her life doesn't exist in these speakers' collected memories of her. And, except for a few scant sentences on the civil rights websites and microfiche articles I looked over this past week, neither does he in historical documents. Their love has been excised from history.

That is what pains me now. I ache not only because of her death— she has lived a life longer than anyone could reasonably expect—but because, with her gone, her story might never be told. Her and John Pressman's love story will be forgotten, except it cannot be. It is up to me now, yet how do I do this when Molly is no longer there to guide me?

She didn't provide me with a list of her colleagues who knew her pre-1961, and, when I checked online, the lack of an internet presence of the people in her story tells me they too have passed on. Even if I can find some folks on Google, will there be anyone there on the other end, sound of body and especially of mind, when I phone? Therein lies the catch-22 of the situation. Catch-22—a term that hadn't even been invented when Molly was my age.

After the service, I exit the chapel, out into the fresh air and the early-August Californian sunshine, but I enjoy neither as my troubling thoughts swirl. A few people with microphones—the only folks my age who were in the chapel—are interviewing the attendees. Reporters, I guess, and I think of the serge-suit-wearing, Buddy-Holly-resembling ones from Molly's tale. The ones waiting at The Porky Pie diner, with their ancient rangefinder cameras, at the beginning of the whole story. The story that I don't know how to end.

"How can I finish the book?" I ask myself, as I head to the parking lot. The entire tale had been in Molly's head for she kept no diary, and there are no letters either since both she and John Pressman were inseparable since the night they first made love. To end the story, I would have to, in essence, make it up. It seems the only solution available.

But then my book—no, *Molly's book*—will no longer be a memoir but a novel. Without a real-life person backing up the tale as truth, the love story, so enchanting and almost otherworldly, could be dismissed as preposterous in this 21st-century world of the internet, reality TV, and 24/7 cynicism. Didn't even I, who heard it straight from Molly herself, first dismiss her story as being too fantastical to be true?

See the magic beneath the everyday, find happiness by helping people, life is an adventure—Molly and John's exhortations no longer seem to possess some overlooked, deeper truth but instead appear unhappily like banalities in every self-help book ever published and with as much connection to the daily lives of regular people.

Except that isn't true. I feel them, those wonderful lessons, myself. Or, at least, I *felt* them. As I near my car, I'm not sure of anything anymore.

Maybe as a consequence of my confusion, I suddenly encounter this nauseating self-pity, and I know it is pathetic even as I feel it. I am going to drive back to my small apartment and failed dreams—the inescapably mediocre life that I find myself in at middle age. Everyone I know, including friends from college and even before, feels trapped in a lightless cave of indeterminate dimensions. But, for a few precious weeks with Molly, I felt I wasn't.

She *did* show me the adventure in the everyday. I am sure of it. But that enlightenment seemed to only exist when she was alive. I am forced to admit that, without her presence, I likely will never understand the magic that she felt when she was with John. Or, for that matter, what I experienced myself these past few weeks.

In this dark mood, I am just opening the door to my car when I hear someone call from behind me, "RC."

RC? Nobody has called me by that name since I graduated from high school. Nobody, that is, except Molly Valle, and I whirl around, expecting a miracle. Of course, it isn't Molly standing there. Instead, I see an elderly African-American woman dressed in a black skirt suit. She is walking haltingly across the parking lot toward me with the help of a cane. I vaguely remember seeing her inside the funeral parlor.

"Yes," I say and also remember that she wasn't one of the speakers.

"You're Molly's biographer, right?" she says and holds out her hand.

"Yes," I say and shake her hand, finding her grip far stronger than suggested by her gait and cane. "How do you—?"

"I'm Bethanee."

Bethanee. I know I've heard the name before, but I stupidly cannot connect it with this old lady's face. Then I remember: *Bethanee Avery.*

I think I stepped back one or two steps. I am not sure since I feel that I've disconnected from my own body. My mental image of Bethanee (young, saucy, wrapped in stylish clothes) and the real-life Bethanee standing in front of me (a white-haired lady dressed in funereal black) are too far apart, as if I were squinting across an impossibly wide gorge. This is not even mentioning the imaginary Bethanee who died in Molly's made-up story.

But I know now that Bethanee didn't come out of the Greyhound bus first that horrible morning in 1961. John did. That is what made all the difference in the world. That is why Bethanee Avery is standing in front of me, in southern California, over a half-century after the fact.

"Oh, my God," I say, and she smiles knowingly, as if she expected that very reaction.

CHAPTER 25

RC

"I looked for you, but I couldn't find you."

"You were looking for Bethanee Avery, right?"

"Yes."

"My last name hasn't been Avery since my wedding forty years ago." She must've noticed something on my face for she adds, "How hopelessly bourgeois of me, right?"

I smile, but that gesture only comes because I don't know what else to do. My life has taken such a fantastical turn these past several weeks, I sometimes think I dreamed it all up. But here, in this elegant, aged lady, is confirmation that it had all been real.

Not that Bethanee looks remotely like her twentysomething self. She is in her late seventies, after all, and looks it—wrinkled and ample, a half-century of living separating her from the unlined, sharp-elbowed girl she once was. Only her eyes, whose punchy directness would be characterized in the '60s as impudence, and the fact that she knows seemingly everything about Molly Valle prove to me that she *is* Bethanee Avery and not some actress in a sick prank whose motivation eludes me.

Even the mundaneness of our present location adds to the unreality. We're in a Starbucks a few blocks from the mortuary. I am sipping my iced green latte, and, across the table, Bethanee is sipping her Teavana Earl Grey.

"I didn't hear you speak at the service," I say.

"I didn't need to," Bethanee says. "Molly's book will speak for me."

"So, she told you about the book."

"Of course. She told me all about it and about you too."

This takes me aback. "How?"

"Over the phone."

The obviousness makes me smile, and she smiles back. She is drinking her tea with precise, never-wasted movements, and I can at last see that *cool* aspect about her. In Molly's story, the young woman was the epitome of cool, and Bethanee as an old woman is cool in much the same way.

She is cool in the manner that only someone from the 1960s can be cool, without the requisite adornments or actions of 21st-century so-called cool. The two-hour gym sessions needed for that perfect body, the porcelain veneers for those perfect teeth, the 24/7 social media obsession to flaunt those assets. No, Bethanee didn't— *doesn't*—need any of that. She has genuine coolness, like what Molly had.

And I realize something I should've seen earlier.

"You're her executor, aren't you?" I ask. "You were the one who arranged for the funeral and sent out the notices."

"I did. Well, my husband and I. We were both glad to do it when she asked us to. We owe the world to her."

Her husband knew Molly too? Then I get it: the shy, straitlaced boy who had a crush on Bethanee—William Graham. The young man whose humiliation Molly stopped at The Porky Pie diner. So everything worked out for him, I think to myself and inwardly smile. He got the girl.

"I didn't see him at the service," I say.

"He's back at the hotel. Didn't want to come, you know? Said it would've felt like a flaming poker through his eye to be there."

After an appropriate silence, I ask, "Where is Molly now?"

"She requested to be cremated," Bethanee says. "In about a week or so, I will send her into the Mississippi River by her hometown."

"Is that where John is?"

"Yes. Finally, they will be together forever."

I absorb this then say, "You're the only one, as far as I can tell, who knew them both."

"Oh, you'll be surprised how many of us are left, rattling teeth and all. I'll email you a list of folks. You should have enough to finish the book then."

I nod, but I am not sure at all. It's one thing to interview people about a singular event, quite another when recreating a real-life love story. Still, I do want to know one thing, and the old lady in front of me can answer it for me.

"You were there, weren't you?"

"Yes, I was," Bethanee says, and for once, her eyes aren't on mine. We both know what the "there" referred to. "Not a single day goes by when I don't think about that moment. We never talked about it, you know? Molly and I."

Then she tells me what happened. It is a tale I've already read on the internet and on microfiche, those reprocessed newspaper accounts from that day, but hearing it from someone who experienced it in the flesh brings a layer of gooseflesh to my skin. The bus ride that Alabaman morning, the gunshot, and the aftermath, captured in horrid permanence by the black and white photograph.

"If John hadn't been there," Bethanee says, her eyes on me again, "if he, in fact, hadn't *pushed* me back inside the bus, I would've been the first one out."

"You must've been so brave."

"Brave?" She shakes her head, her still full head of white curls bouncing. "No, I wasn't brave. I was an aloof little bitch who was actually scared out of her mind. And I would've done something reckless just to prove to myself that I wasn't scared. John saved me from that. John and Molly both. Do you understand that?"

"Yes."

"You know what's amazing?" Bethanee says. "Rather than separate us, John's passing bound Molly and me together like conjoined twins. We were completely inseparable for the next decade or so, all throughout the civil rights movement."

"Can you tell me what happened?"

Bethanee does, and I sit forward, mesmerized. Some of the stories were told at the memorial service, but others are unknown to me. A very small part, no doubt, of the treasure chest of experiences that she and Molly accumulated in the insane, cruel, glorious decade that was the 1960s. I hear her words, and in my mind, I *see* them.

I see Molly and Bethanee among the throngs at the Washington Memorial in '63, their faces sweat-glazed and radiant as Martin Luther King steps to the podium. I see Molly and Bethanee under an enormous spruce pine, teaching a semi-circle of kids in the backwaters of the Mississippi Delta in '64. I see Molly and Bethanee, linked arm in arm with other demonstrators, as they cross a bridge to meet a phalanx of billy-club-tapping Alabaman deputies in '65. I see Molly and Bethanee in meetings, in riots, in rallies, in jail cells, across the chaos-dotted parabola of the 1960s, long ago yet not too long at all, William Faulkner being right, the past not ever leaving us, the past not even the past.

Two women, one middle-aged going on old, the other young going on middle-aged, yet both somehow ageless and consummately heroic. Neither wealthy nor famous but living lives that were richer, more meaningful, and more exciting than those of billionaires and movie stars. Lives so dazzling, I feel my eyes moistening as I listen to Bethanee Avery.

"Only in the early '70s, when the dust had settled a bit, did we finally part. Molly to live near her brother here in California, and me, well, I decided to move to New Orleans. Even became a social worker, which is what I did for thirty-five years. Working for a state government I once despised. Ain't that a trip? I became the sellout my younger, dumber self always ranted about."

Bethanee smiles and sips more of her tea.

"You know, back then, I always thought I could control fate," she continues. "But now, as I've become a wizened old sage, I realize Molly and John had always been right. The sad truth is lives are controlled by fate and often by the ugliest fate. That's why you have to tell their story. To strike back against that cruel fate."

I'm about to put forth an objection when I realize I understand what she means. Slowly, very slowly, I begin to see the spine of the story, and for the first time, I think I can indeed finish the book. I can also see the ending of the story, like a landscape finally being revealed by lifting mist.

However, I also recognize something else, something unexpected. I don't want the story to end.

"What's the matter?" Bethanee asks.

I wonder if I should tell her, but then I realize I don't quite understand it myself. I just have a vague foreboding that the rest of my life will be like walking a plank off a pirate ship.

"When Molly began telling me her story a few weeks ago," I finally say, "I felt good about my life again. Really good. For the first time, really, in a long time. But now that she's gone, I feel … I don't know, adrift. Does that make sense?"

"No longer seeing the beauty and adventure behind the everyday, right?"

"Yes!" I say, far too loudly in the coffee shop, causing a couple of bristly hipsters to glance over. I don't care at all. I ask Bethanee, "She told you too, huh?"

"Mm-hmm, when I was twenty-five. But, speaking only for myself, I didn't quite buy it till I was older."

"Older when?"

"When I was in my mid-fifties or so." She laughs, and I guess if I could see my own stupefied face, I would've too. "So you have another decade of groping in the dark ahead of you, I'm afraid."

I try to smile, but it doesn't come. Bethanee's prediction has somewhat dampened my initial elation. I don't want to live another decade as bewildering and meaningless as my previous one.

"I guess if I have to wait, I have to wait," I say, resigned. "But I just don't know if I will ever live that adventurous life or even fully believe what Molly said."

"Why not?"

"I guess it's because you and Molly are, well, heroes. And I'm not."

"Oh, no, you are too," Bethanee says.

My headshake is automatic. Whatever adjectives could be used to describe my life so far, "heroic" isn't one of them.

"No, you are," Bethanee insists. "I'm not blowing smoke up your ass, RC."

I laugh then—a genuine laugh that feels damn good. Of course, it's not uncommon for old ladies to curse, I guess. She is, after all, *Bethanee Avery*, albeit a much older version.

"You're a teacher, aren't you?" she asks me. "Don't tell me you haven't sacrificed during all those years in the classroom. Stop and think."

I am about to object again when I shut up and take her advice. I stop and think.

"I'm going to, as they used to say back in my day, powder my nose."

Bethanee stands up, turns, and heads to the restroom. I watch her go then stare at her empty seat for a few moments. Nothing comes at first but coffee-shop white noise. Inane conversations, tapping keyboards, whirring blenders. But then it does come to me, like waking up to blazing sunshine through a drapeless window, and I wonder how I could've missed it all these years.

I think of all the inner-city schools in the Los Angeles Unified School District where I've worked during my twenty-year teaching career. Roosevelt High School in Boyle Heights, John Liechty Middle School west of downtown, and finally, my current school, Orthopedic Medical Magnet in South LA. I think of all my classes, both the good ones and the Looney Tunes ones, and the late afternoons I spent grading papers at my desk, my sole reprieve being hourly stretches before the open window, admiring the smog-enhanced sunsets of LA.

I think of all those students who still keep in contact with me. Brian Ochoa, whose college entrance essay I helped compose, a bizarre homage to Matthew McConaughey that nonetheless got him into Yale. Shantel Wells, who entered my remedial English class her freshman year, went for years to my thrice-weekly after-school tutoring, and entered my AP English course as a senior. Fatima Mahfouz, whose filmmaking dreams I encouraged when nobody else did, whose screenplay years later won her a screenwriting competition at USC Film School and a three-picture deal at DreamWorks.

The barely restrained chaos and the unexpected laughter in my out-of-control classes, the countless dive bars I frequented with other teachers, the short-lived but dazzling affairs I had with some female colleagues ... all those memories I've long forgotten come back to me now with a jolt. How did they slip from my memory? Why have I considered the last twenty years of my life a black hole from which nothing good could've escaped?

Of course, I know the answer. I went into teaching as a stepping stone to my writing career, and when that fizzled and died, I was cut adrift and so very resentful. How does that John Lennon song go? "Life is what happens to you while you're busy making other plans." That was me. I was so angry and frustrated by my failed writing ambitions, I couldn't see my life as a teacher being fulfilling in its own right. I missed it—but now I see it.

I see it.

Bethanee is back. "Well, do you understand it a bit more?" she asks as she sits down.

"I sort of do, but—"

"There is no but. Folks don't give themselves enough credit. The mother who endures cavities so her children can get braces. The father who works a dead-end job so his kids can have a roof over their heads. The daughter who sacrifices college so she can take care of her disabled mother. They are all heroes, and don't you believe otherwise."

"Maybe," I say but can't stop the frown that emerges. "But those— well, maybe I should say, *my* so-called heroics. Don't they seem so paltry next to yours and Molly's? I mean, you two lived through the civil rights era, for God's sakes."

"True. But we didn't fight the Nazis either."

"What does that mean?"

"It means every single generation venerates the one before it. John Steinbeck once wrote that America used to be a so-called 'nation of giants' but not anymore. That was in *Travels with Charley*, which was published in 1960, before I'd even met Molly. But just because Steinbeck said it doesn't mean the idea's correct because it's not."

I say nothing, trying in vain to connect Bethanee's dots, which are like billiard balls after a hard break.

"What I'm trying to say is," she continues, "you are living in a time of great adventure, just like I did during the civil rights era. Just like my parents did through the Great Depression and World War II. A hundred years from now, folks will look back at this time period and think, Wow, what an incredible moment it must've been to be alive. Syrian refugees, human trafficking, climate change—the whole world is out there waiting to be saved. And you'll have a grand adventure doing it, even if only in what you consider a small, locally based way. You know, you already have as a teacher."

"I just didn't look deeply enough, right?" I ask and smile.

"That's right. You just need to understand that each day has its own possibilities."

I nod hesitantly and want to dwell a bit on her words. But I don't have the time as Bethanee checks her watch and says, "Can you drive me back, RC? My husband's picking me up in ten minutes."

We are both quiet on the five-minute ride back to the mortuary, and I turn her words over and over again in my mind. Then, before I know it, we are both standing by my car. We exchange phone numbers and email addresses. She promises me that she will email me that list of people who knew Molly and John.

"If you ever get lost in the woods, just contact me. My husband and I'll come to your rescue. Narratively speaking, at least. Speaking of which, here he comes."

I don't know what to expect, maybe a black Lincoln Town Car or something equally stereotypical that old timers drive. But the vehicle entering the parking lot is a red Toyota Prius.

What is more surprising, though, is that the driver is most assuredly *not* William Graham. For one thing, he's not African American. I see a pale, lined face behind the steering wheel. A bald head supported by a thick neck and wide, cantaloupe-shaped shoulders. I step back a bit, the realization hitting me like an immense, invisible boxing glove.

I recall a half-century-old conversation Bethanee had with Molly, when she informed her that an unexpected visitor had come to one of their meetings. The gentle, overgrown, mathematically inclined boy who wanted to be an engineer but instead, under parental and social pressure, became a small-town sheriff like his father. At least, in Molly's fabricated tale to me.

"Your last name," I say slowly, turning to Bethanee. "It wouldn't be ..."

"Harper," she says, nodding. "I'm Bethanee Harper now. Yes, I'm cavorting with the blue-eyed white devil. What *would* my younger self ever think of me?"

As she chuckles, the Prius parks beside my car. The old man opens the door and comes up to us, grinning an enormous gap-toothed grin.

"How are you, RC?" He shakes my hand. "I'm Cash."

I mumble "fine" or something or other. Then I ask the only question that's on my mind: "Did you ever become an engineer?"

Cash and Bethanee exchange looks then laugh together.

"You betcha," Molly's old student tells me. "Retired just this past year. Rockwell Semiconductors."

And I think, *Here is another of her miracles.*

CHAPTER 26

RC

It is the second decade of the 21st century, and I am forty-four years old. I am driving on the 405 Freeway from Orange County back to my home in Los Angeles. I am in a world altogether different from the one I inhabited in my mind as I listened to Bethanee Harper, née Avery, tell her story. And, for once, I don't mind. Her world has moved on, but my world ... well, I'm still living in it.

The sun is an intense spotlight in the sky, and I am sweating buckets, my rattling Hyundai's air-con having gone on the fritz months ago. Just like my small, ground-floor apartment's central air. But, again, I don't mind. Nor do I care about the smog-thick air I'm breathing in or even my multitudinous failures, both professional and personal, in life.

See, I learned something from Molly, a lesson that Bethanee only reinforced. I am merely at the midway point in the novel of my own life. On around page 250 of a 500-page tale and, given future medical advances, maybe even 200. There's no reason why the next 250, 300, or even 350 pages will not be far more exciting than the first half.

Once back in my apartment, I will go online and research the story. I will be going back half a century again, and when Bethanee emails me the list of acquaintances tonight, I will start calling those people tomorrow. In a couple of weeks, I will go with Bethanee and Cash to Molly's Mississippi town and have them show me the locations where Molly and John's story took place. Molly's old house, the dorm rooms at Jupiter Hammon College, even where The Porky Pie diner used to be. But Bethanee warned me, "It's boarded up, like the rest of downtown. It's all Walmarts and Targets on the town's outskirts now."

As I drive, I think of those Walmarts and Targets, the most pedestrian of stores, and how they were constructed near a location that once held the most amazing love story. A love story that, I understand now, has no end. Love is eternal—something I should've learned from Molly, who learned it from John, who learned it from God knows who. There is no end to that kind of love, even if the lovers' bodies ceased to exist. That love is manifested everywhere else, in a million other couples worldwide, and probably a few not far from where I am driving, up the freeway, through a world I thought I knew but admit that I don't know at all.

"Each day has its own possibilities," Bethanee told me, and I think of those words as my dashboard GPS shows the freeway lanes turning bright red from my present location all the way to the exit to my apartment complex, fully six miles away.

I veer off an exit ramp, intending to take surface streets home, the pleasant female voice of the GPS protesting that I'm not taking the shortest possible route home. I turn the machine off and absurdly feel like Luke Skywalker in his X-wing fighter at the end of *Star Wars*. The liberation I feel is real, but there's a certain discomfort too. I've so overly planned my life and so berated myself for falling short of that plan, I don't know how to act in its absence.

I'm passing through a predominantly Latino neighborhood. Spanish-language store signs ("Farmacia," "Pescaderia," "Tortilleria"), sidewalk fruit and tamale stands, cowboy-hat-wearing men riding BMX bicycles, Catholic-uniformed schoolgirls with faces glued to smartphones. It is the Lower East Side updated to modern-day Los Angeles. And it is a view that I, as an Angeleno of two decades, have seen countless times before, with no more interest in than a rerun of *Wheel of Fortune*. Or so I thought before.

Yet, as I stop at a familiar intersection, I suddenly hear music. It is Latin music, but beyond that, I have no idea what it is. But it sounds classical in nature and unlike what I heard at a recent *quinceañera* that I was invited to. No, this is like what accompanied the folk dances that I've observed in Mexico City on a holiday. The music is also incongruously coming from a cookie-cutter, beige-stucco building to my right.

Possibilities to be grasped.

At this stoplight, one I've idled at seemingly a million times before, I do something different. I turn my steering wheel and drive into the beige building's parking lot. I exit my car and head toward the building, whose sign reads, "Bienvenidos Community Center."

Inside, the air conditioning and lively music both hit me like a delectable breeze from another, better world.

I am in a dimmed auditorium, with a couple hundred people sitting on folding chairs before me, staring and clapping at the lit stage where a trio of young girls, dressed in white blouses and ruffled black skirts, are tapping and spinning away to the music. *Folklorico*—the word comes to me from somewhere. That's what the girls, all around twelve, are dancing. Grinning, seemingly inexhaustible, their whirling torsos and limbs perfectly in sync with unseen guitars, violins, and trumpets.

"Can I help you?"

I turn to my left and see a fetching, friendly-looking woman around my age. She is standing behind a table, which my daylight-shrunken pupils missed when I first stepped into the darkened room. The nametag on her teal T-shirt reads, "Veronika."

"Yes," I say and give her my name. Then I add, "I drive by this place at least once a week and didn't know what it was. Today, I heard music and decided to stop by."

"Well, I'm glad you came," Veronika says and smiles. In lightly accented English, she proceeds to explain what Bienvenidos is—a community center that provides job fairs, a food bank, women's health services …

As she speaks, I look into her brown eyes, and I suddenly feel like I can see her whole life behind her. Growing up on the outskirts of San Jose, Costa Rica, the only child of travel guides, who took folks to the biodiverse wonderlands that were the nearby rivers. In sunshine and rain, which often came in brief cloudbursts that almost soaked through their small boat's canvas roof, her parents explained to the tourists—and also to her, for she was always there, sitting rapt in the stern—the reptiles and mammals of their land. The caterwauling howler monkeys, the lurking caimans, and, most of all, the countless birds whose feathers were so splashy, it was as if they'd flown through a room of exploding paint cans. She took her love of animals with her to the *universidad*, where she graduated with a biology degree a few years before her family immigrated to Los Angeles and she became a high school science teacher.

A teacher like me. I see my stars beginning to align.

Except they never get there. For I know that one of those dancing kids is Veronika's own daughter, the result of a happy marriage between her and her husband, a fellow teacher at their school. An immense man of boundless self-confidence; a lover of In-N-Out Burgers, archery and fishing, and pre-Columbian cultures. Everything that I'm not and never will be.

But I don't mind. Not too much anyway. I am instead transfixed by what I am seeing, this woman's life in front of me. Is it truth or is it fiction? Then I hear Molly asking me, "Does it matter? Do you actually think this woman has no stories to tell?" Of course, she does. Everyone in this auditorium does. A million stories to be drawn out, to be relived, to be experienced and loved. A million stories so close to home, and, all these years, I didn't even know it.

"Do you take volunteers?" I ask Veronika once she's finished her description of the center. "Maybe on the weekends? I'm an English teacher."

"Oh, great, we love teachers. On Saturdays, we provide translation services here. You would just need to fill this out."

She hands me a volunteer application and asks if I want to sit down. I shake my head and tell her that I'll return the application tomorrow. Then I say I'll best be going, and when the song and dance end and the audience claps, I proceed to do just that. At the door, however, I find myself turning and asking her, "You don't happen to also be a teacher, right?"

"Why, yes, I am. Chemistry teacher at Garfield High School. Where do you teach?"

I tell her my school then say goodbye. I walk out into the afternoon sun and blink at the blinding sunlight. But the image of Veronika stays with me, and I smile to myself. Not so much because of *her* but because of the possibilities that I now perceive in front of me and my life, like a freshly paved road that proceeds past all the magnificent landmarks of the world.

"Thank you," I say to Molly Valle as I start up my car. "Thank you, thank you, thank you."

As I drive out of the parking lot to go home, I think:

Magic exists. It really does. And I'm on a great adventure.

ABOUT THE AUTHOR

Ray Smith lives in Los Angeles and is
working on another book.

He can be contacted at
themagnoliathatbloomedunseen.com

Made in United States
Orlando, FL
06 April 2022

16540268R00146